I0716321

MURDER ON THE COLORADO

A Fen Maguire Mystery

MURDER ON THE COLORADO

A Fen Maguire Mystery

BRUCE HAMMACK

To my long time friend, Janet. You have shared your table (and your encouragement) with me more times than I can count. And to your mother, Eloise, who taught you well. Thank you for loaning me her name for this book.

To my new friends, Tiffany and Joe. You have taken a place to stay the night and turned it into a 'home away from home' with your warmth and ability to make a stranger feel like a friend.

Chapter One

It's not every day you see a kayak dragging a lifeless body toward shore.

Fen looked up from his sketch pad and took in the bizarre scene. A small flotilla of kayaks in a variety of colors approached a clearing on the banks of the Colorado River. Excited voices skipped across the ambling body of water that seemed too sleepy to bother with the grim goings-on.

Fen stuffed his artist's pencil into the pocket of his shirt as he focused on the only green kayak. Most of the boats reached shore before the one with a rope tied around the face-down figure. That kayak, like the river, took its time.

Quick steps brought him down from a concrete observation platform that overlooked the muddy ribbon of water with towering trees and thick foliage on both banks. Willing hands lifted and pulled the body onto the shore as Fen scurried down the riverbank.

He reached semi-level ground and took a better look at the kayaks. There were eight, and they each held a large, clear, plastic bag partially filled with trash. Everyone in the group wore matching shirts emblazoned with *Keep The Colorado Trash Free.*

"Leave him there and don't turn him over," said the man piloting the green kayak. His voice had the tone of authority, like someone who was used to giving orders and expected them to be carried out.

The man slipped out of his life vest. Sweat stained both the front and back of his T-shirt. Salt and pepper hair poked out from under a baseball cap emblazoned with a logo Fen didn't recognize. He looked at a woman and barked out like a drill sergeant, "Bonnie, did you call the police?"

"Not yet. My phone is in my dry bag. It was way behind me. You know how nervous I get when I'm on the water. I didn't want to reach for it for fear of tipping—"

The man cut her off. "Who has a blasted phone?" Under his breath, he added, "Of all days to leave it in my truck."

Fen spoke in a voice that carried. "I'll make the call."

The man shot him an accusatory look. "Who the heck are you?"

"Someone who knows how to talk to 911 dispatchers."

"That doesn't tell me a single thing. Give me your phone and I'll call."

Fen shrugged, closed the distance, and held out his phone. "Be my guest."

The man punched in three numbers and turned his back. Fen heard only one side of the conversation as the man pressed the phone hard against his ear. "I just pulled a dead man out of the river... No, I don't know his name... My name is Riley Eastham...What kind of stupid question is that? The Colorado River... The park with baseball fields and rodeo grounds... That's right, there's a raised concrete platform at the top of the bank and a parking lot for cars. Get someone out here quick."

He hung up the phone and was in the process of sticking it

in his pocket when Fen extended his hand. The phone came back to its rightful owner. It rang within seconds of him reclaiming it.

"This is Fen Maguire."

"Bastrop County 911. I'm verifying a call we received a few moments ago came from this number. Did you make it?"

"It came from my phone, but I wasn't the one who called."

"The caller said something about a body in the river?"

"That's correct. He reported a body he brought to shore at the park on the outskirts of Smithville. It's where the bridge crosses over Highway 71." Fen took a breath. "By the way, I'm the former sheriff of Newman County. I can confirm this is a suspicious death, and this location is not the original crime scene. You'll need to contact the sheriff's department, City of Smithville P.D., and the state game warden. I'm sure state troopers will want to look, too."

"Thanks, Sheriff. Help's on the way."

The call ended, but Riley Eastham's blustering continued. "You should have told me you were a former sheriff." His face clouded with a question. "Why did you tell the dispatcher to send cops from four different departments? Isn't one enough?"

"The body was in the river, right?"

"Yeah."

"Any crime occurring on a state river falls under the jurisdiction of the Department of Public Safety. That means game wardens and state troopers. If this turns out to be a homicide, the jurisdictional lines may get blurred. Let's say the original crime scene is in the city of Smithville. The city police will need to investigate. If, however, the original crime scene is outside the city limits, the sheriff's department will be investigating."

"That's inefficient."

"Perhaps, but it works unless the various departments don't get along."

A wailing siren approached but was still some distance off. The booming voice of Riley Eastham sounded like a bullhorn as he turned to his team. "Don't just stand there. Get the trash off your kayaks and into larger bags. I have things to do today."

Fen spoke in his best cop voice. "Don't touch anything. What you collected today is evidence until you're told otherwise. First responders will soon be here and will need to take statements from you. The best thing you can do is get away from this area." He pointed toward the bank. "Go to the platform and wait."

Riley spun and stared. Fen pulled the corners of his mouth up into a smile. "Just a suggestion, Mr. Eastham."

Half-closed eyes showed displeasure, but Riley saved a little face by bellowing out. "You heard him. Go to the platform and wait."

"Can I get my phone?" asked Bonnie.

"No," snapped Riley. "You missed your chance to get it out of your dry bag when you were on the river."

Everyone made it to the platform before a City of Smithville police car arrived, and mercifully turned off the blaring siren. Fen determined that the officer in this city of four thousand souls didn't run with lights and sirens often. Given the opportunity, he made the most of it. The man in uniform bounded out of the car and asked, "Is Sheriff Maguire here?"

Fen raised his hand. "Former sheriff," but followed it with, "Your name tag reads West. What's your first name?"

"John."

"Well, John West, you'll want to talk to Mr. Eastham. He brought the body to shore and knows much more about this than I do."

The officer gave a nod of recognition to the man who

appeared to be the leader of the group wearing identical shirts. "Good morning, Mr. Eastham. If you and Sheriff Maguire would come with me, I'd appreciate it."

Riley led the way down the riverbank. He stopped about ten feet from the body and spoke in a soft, almost reverent voice. "He was in the water about three hundred yards east of the Highway 230 bridge."

Fen asked, "Were you the one who spotted the body?"

"Yeah. I was leading the others, going from one riverbank to the other, pointing out pockets of trash that needed to be picked up."

It was then that Fen noticed the bag in Riley's boat had significantly less trash than the others. "Which bank was he near?"

"The north bank, away from town. There must be something under the water that makes it swirl. Trash gathers there. Only today, it wasn't all plastic bottles, beer cans, and everything else you can imagine."

Too late, Fen realized he'd overstepped his authority by asking questions. He looked at the young officer and gave an almost imperceptible nod. The officer took over. "Mr. Eastham, you can return to the platform. I'd like to speak to Sheriff Maguire alone."

A grumbling Riley Eastham trudged up the riverbank. Fen and the young officer turned toward the river. In a hushed tone, John led off with a question. "What do you recommend I do first?"

Fen ran a hand down his face. "How long have you been out of the training academy?"

"Five weeks."

"Do you have crime scene tape?"

"A fresh roll. I've never had to use it before."

"There's a first time for everything." He lifted his head.

"Those sirens tell me help is on the way. Do these two things: Tell everyone from the trash pickup team that they're not free to leave. I seriously doubt you'll be the one to take their statements, but each one will need to give a statement before they can be released. Next, get the tape up as quickly as possible. That will save you from getting chewed out for forgetting the first things they taught you to do with a crime scene."

The young officer swallowed. "Anything else?"

"Your supervisor will probably tell you to move to the street that leads to the parking lot. Expect a long, boring day of allowing emergency vehicles through, but no civilians. If you don't have a few bottles of water, there's some in my truck I'll give you."

A groan came from the young officer. "They told me to do that in training. I was in a hurry this morning and forgot."

"You'll remember the next time."

The sound of tires coming to a sudden stop sounded from over the steep embankment. Fen didn't envy the long, hot day the officer would have. The late June sun was rising over the trees and a sweltering riverbank wasn't his idea of a place to spend the rest of the morning, let alone the afternoon.

Oh well, at least this wasn't his case. He estimated his stay by the river might last another hour. Two at the most. Then, he'd enjoy a leisurely lunch in an air-conditioned restaurant. He'd follow that with a nice, long drive in the country. Perhaps the manager of The Katy House Bed and Breakfast would allow him to check in early and he'd get in a nap. It was worth a phone call.

Chapter Two

F en noticed one of the trash pickers, a man with a full head of gray hair, pull his phone out to take a phone call. The man walked down from the raised platform and approached the group of lawmen gathered near the body. "I need to talk to whoever's in charge."

"What do you need, Dr. Fox?" asked a city policeman with captain bars on his collar.

"Doobie Rusk's mule kicked him in the mouth. He's been to the emergency room. They referred him to me to see if I can save his front teeth. He's on his way to my office."

A voice came from over Fen's shoulder. "Let him go. He came to spy on me for his momma, not to pick up trash."

Riley Eastham peered down from the platform, his hands gripping the rail.

The police captain shifted his gaze from Riley to the man Fen assumed to be a dentist. "You can leave, Clayton, but I'll need a statement from you today. Call me when you're free and I'll send an officer to interview you."

Fen's questioning gaze was enough to prompt the captain to speak. "Clayton's the town's only dentist."

"Riley Eastham doesn't seem to be a fan."

"The feeling is mutual."

The desire to ask more questions almost set Fen's tongue in motion. Almost, but not quite. He let the unspoken questions remain that way as he felt the first bead of sweat run down his side. Word must have spread that a former sheriff was involved. Volunteer firefighters and a curious constable with a belly that hung well over his belt joined the crowd that outnumbered the trash pickers. This led Fen to believe that major crimes were rare in Smithville, Texas. The beauty and barber shops would be abuzz with a combination of truths, half-truths, and embellishments by the time he found a restaurant with a decent hamburger.

The relatively cool morning had morphed into a humid, seemingly airless afternoon. The game warden was the last to arrive and made his belated appearance in a flat-bottom metal boat powered by an outboard motor. By this time, Fen had spoken with officers and supervisors from every other department he'd mentioned to Riley Eastham.

The game warden exited the front of his boat and tied the bow line to a tree. Fen immediately recognized him. Ben Crump nodded greetings to others wearing uniforms of various descriptions, then focused on Fen. The two shook hands. Ben had a Central Texas drawl thick as molasses on a frosty day. "Howdy, Fen."

Fen nodded back. "It's been a while. How's Martha and the kids?"

"The youngest is finally out of A&M and Martha's taking a belly-dancing class at the community college. I'm not sure if she lost her mind or is going through some sort of crisis. She bought the entire costume, including a metal belt with all kinds of things that jingle-jangle."

A hearty laugh spurted out of Fen's mouth. "You landed a keeper when you talked her into marrying you."

"That's a fact."

With the preliminaries out of the way, a few seconds of silence followed before Ben asked, "What's the story about the body?"

"A man named Riley Eastham found the body upstream on the north side of the river."

Ben huffed in a way that communicated he knew Riley. Fen gave him the approximate location of where Riley found the body.

"I know the spot. It always collects trash. Passed it on the way here. Had to put in at the boat ramp under the 230 bridge. Has anyone identified the victim?"

"The justice of the peace had EMS turn him over. Everyone looked, but no one recognized him. It could be because he's been on the bottom for a long time. No wallet or other I.D. on him. They bagged the body and hauled it off about an hour ago."

"What was he wearing?"

"Jeans, boots, a black T-shirt."

Ben looked toward the river. "That narrows it down to half the population in the county. Well, it's better than finding a body stripped down to their birthday suit."

Fen gave his old friend another ray of hope. "I took some pictures of Riley dragging the body behind his kayak. I'll send them to you. You can add them to the photos taken by a city patrolman."

Ben nodded his thanks. "It's going to take a lot more than photographs to solve this one. I'm expecting some sort of multijurisdictional task force." He sighed. "I'm too near retirement to endure any more of those."

Fen extended his hand. "Good luck. I can honestly say I'm glad it's you and not me."

At that moment, a horse fly dined on Fen's neck. He slapped it, resulting in a large stain on the palm of his hand. Ben chuckled. "Serves you right for not volunteering to help me. Don't you want to go upstream and look at where they found the body?"

"Thanks for the invitation, but the only thing I want is a large glass of iced tea and a half-pound burger with fries."

"Try Pockets Grille in town. Great burgers."

"I saw it coming into town. I hope their air conditioner is up and running."

"Are you staying long?"

"Only one night, but I'm coming back in September. The local artists' guild wants me to teach a class on painting landscapes."

"Plan to have supper with me and Martha when you come back." He paused. "Are you still flying solo?"

Fen nodded as a stab of emotional pain hit him. "No change on that and I'm not looking."

Ben offered a hand to shake and placed his left hand on Fen's shoulder. "I don't blame you. Martha's all the woman I could ever hope for. I'm so used up, no one else would want me."

Fen added what he could to lighten the mood. "It's not every man that can come home to a jingling, jangling belly dancer."

Ben's smile parted his lips. "I need to get upstream. It's going to be a long, hot day."

Fen didn't ask permission to leave as he'd already spoken with everyone he needed to. He collected his easel, sketch pad and pencils, and brought his truck to life. On the way out of the park, he passed the youthful officer he'd met hours ago. The young man raised a bottle of water as a salute. Fen turned onto Highway 71, lowered the temp of the air conditioner and pointed the vents his direction. He passed the airport and crossed the bridge spanning the Colorado, one of the longest rivers in Texas. Once past the bridge, it was only a few blocks before he turned left and swung into the parking lot of Pockets Grille. The diminutive size of Smithville made everything only minutes away.

A wave of cool air hit him the moment he opened the restaurant's door. The menu on a wall displayed a variety of items, including hamburgers with snappy names based on the toppings. Fen played it safe and ordered a standard burger with fries. He took a seat and sipped a glass of half-sweet, half-unsweetened iced tea.

His eyes swept across the walls and shelves. Most of the decor dealt with movie memorabilia. Items from the movie *Hope Floats* took center stage. He remembered the movie because it was one of Sally's favorites. Curious how a small Texas town became the location for a major movie, he did a search for Smithville on his phone and discovered the small town had been the location of many other films. The posters and other forms of advertising bore witness to the town's favor with producers and directors.

While he nibbled on the last of his fries, Fen's phone came to life. The screen read *The Katy House*. He answered with the standard hello.

"Mr. Maguire?"

"Yes."

"Eloise from The Katy House. I wanted to let you know that the Texas Special room is ready whenever you want to check in."

The idea of a shower, followed by a nap during the heat of the day, suited Fen down to the soles of his boots. He'd delay looking for other locations to paint landscapes until things cooled off.

"That's good news. I'm at Pockets finishing lunch."

"You're almost within rock-throwing distance. Come whenever you're ready."

The woman wasn't kidding when she said the bed-and-breakfast was nearby. He parked in front of the brick two-story home with a large front porch, complete with a row of four white rocking chairs and an inviting two-person porch swing. A smaller porch came off one of the upstairs bedrooms and faced the quiet street.

As he stepped onto the porch, the front door swung open. "Hello, Mr. Maguire. I'm Lanie. Welcome to The Katy House."

Fen removed his hat and stepped across the threshold into a foyer that could have come out of an historical homes magazine. He set his overnight bag on the floor and allowed his gaze to sweep appreciatively up the staircase, then through the double doorway leading to a living room. After explaining how to use his four-digit front door code, the teenage girl led him through the living room into a nicely appointed dining room, with a table that spanned the length of the room. The owner had managed to keep the warmth of the home's early twentieth century charm, while bringing in modern conveniences. They made the loop back to the foyer where she led him up the staircase to his room. Squeaking wooden stairs led to three bedrooms. Lanie turned right, then opened a door at the end of the hall. "I hope you'll enjoy your stay in our Texas Special room. It's a guest favorite because of its private balcony."

Fen nodded his approval and said, "Very nice." as she gave him a short tour of the room, its en suite bathroom and amenities. He gave a tired sigh as he closed the door behind Lanie.

The spacious room held everything he expected and a few things he didn't. A small refrigerator came stocked with bottles of water and soft drinks. The king bed felt like a cloud and twin wingback chairs sat in front of a massive window, perfect for reading. He swung open the original double doors to the balcony and stepped out. Four wicker chairs and a table would be perfect for enjoying an early morning cup of coffee.

The bathroom boasted vintage fixtures, including an art déco sink and a clawfoot tub. A white shower curtain hung on an oval stainless-steel frame hanging from the ceiling. Fen didn't soak in a tub often, but it was nice to have the option. It occurred to him that he should go downstairs and introduce himself to the proprietor. He took three steps and turned around. The lure of a cool shower and a nap overrode his desire for social interaction. Besides, he'd more than exhausted his daily supply of words with the first responders.

The shower washed away sweat and most of the thoughts of the scene he'd witnessed. It wasn't long before the combination of cool air and clean clothes pulled him onto the bed. He set the alarm function on his phone to allow a two-hour nap. That's the last thing he remembered until the annoying sound of lively AI-generated musical notes roused him from a deep slumber.

He stumbled to the bathroom and splashed cool water on his face. Like it or not, he had to find at least two more locations suitable for students to paint landscapes.

As he dried his face on a fluffy white towel, questions rose to the surface. Was the man in the river a victim of a tragic accident, or was he the victim of a crime? If so, where was the original crime scene? Fen hung the towel on the rack. Either way, the investigation didn't involve him.

Chapter Three

Fen stepped into the dining room, his gaze sweeping appreciatively around the room. One sideboard held a table-top ice maker with bottles of water and glass mason jars for anyone with a thirst to slake. A second side table held a one-cup-at-a-time coffee maker with a collection of white porcelain mugs. Pods of coffee and bags of tea stood at the ready, along with the usual sweeteners and packets of creamers. He made a cup of coffee, hoping the caffeine would wipe away the rest of the sleep-induced cobwebs. Since Thelma, his cook-house-keeper and self-appointed guardian, wasn't here to scold him, he picked up a couple of pieces of chocolate from the candy jar and sat down at the dining room table that could easily seat ten. Maybe twelve if everyone got friendly.

What interested him most was the note the owner had left for him.

You're the only guest staying the night. A friendly warning: the word is out about who you are and how you helped at the river. If you're looking for a place to eat

tonight, try The Front Room Wine Bar. Don't let the name fool you; the menu is limited, but the food is very good. It's two blocks east at 2nd and Main.
Come hungry for breakfast in the morning at 9:00 a.m.

With the summer solstice only a handful of days past, daylight would stay for many hours to come. This meant he had plenty of time to scout for locations to paint. With a small cooler of water already in his truck, he turned left on 2nd Street and located The Front Room Wine Bar. He hoped the unpretentious building held a hidden gem for a place to eat later that evening.

He turned left on Main and drove one block past commercial businesses then turned right on Highway 230, the main road that bisected Smithville.

His impression of the town was that it had stopped growing somewhere between 1930 and 1955. It was refreshing in a nostalgic sort of way to see a town with character that came from years gone by, even if it was like driving his new truck in a time capsule. What tales could this town tell?

Fen's memory flashed to this morning's scene at the river. The town was adding another story that included his name if Eloise's note was anything to go by.

In a burg the size of Smithville, it didn't take long to reach the edge of town. Three miles past the city limit sign, he crossed over Shipp Lake. It was a long, narrow body of water that offered interesting views of both banks. The railroad right-of-way provided an excellent view of the narrow lake. This was site number two for the artists.

He hoped the students had enough sense to realize they couldn't place their easels on the tracks as freight trains frequented Smithville at all hours of the day and night.

Fen turned his truck around and headed northwest toward

Buescher State Park. He'd been there years before with Sally. Early in their marriage they'd gone tent camping, only to have a violent thunderstorm come up in the wee hours. Drenched by the time they ran to the truck, they'd spent the remaining hours trying to sleep in the cramped front seat. What he'd give to spend one more day and night roughing it with her.

A sigh escaped and he put words to his thoughts. "I know you told me to move on, but I can't yet." That last word surprised him. It was something he'd never said before.

Fen looked up toward the heavens. "I'll make a deal with you, Sally. I won't get all blubbery when I go to the place we spent the night if you forget that I said *yet*."

The state park lay two and a half miles north of Smithville. He stopped at the front gate to obtain a day pass and a map. The latter revealed points of interest, including a thirty-acre lake. There were campsites with or without, electricity and water hookups, as well as screened-in shelters and a smattering of cabins. Hiking trails through the thousand-acre park were also clearly marked, as was the twelve-mile driving/biking road.

His first stop was at the lake where he parked and walked. He saw in his mind's eye at least five aspiring artists spread out along the bank, sketching and painting. He returned to his truck and followed the asphalt road through dense woods that boasted hilly terrain, thick woods, and towering loblolly pines. Most of the terrain seemed too dense to offer a distant view, but there were a few spots that could work.

The road looped back to more campsites. He slowed and came to a stop at the one where he and Sally had pitched their tiny tent and spent a gloriously miserable night. Back then tents might withstand a short rain shower, but not a full-blown storm.

He expected the campsite to be vacant, but it wasn't. Two bicycles stood in front of a tent that reminded him of the one he threw away as soon as they returned home. Lawn chairs held a brown-haired man and a blond woman who couldn't have been over twenty years of age. They sat with their backs to the road, seemingly looking into their future.

The lump in Fen's throat felt like a golf ball. He closed his eyes, mainly to keep them from leaking. It didn't work.

Without thinking about what he was doing, he put the truck in gear and allowed it to ease forward. It had been a long time since he missed his wife this much. A therapist had told him time would heal his grief. "Not yet," he said to himself.

"There it is again. Another, 'not yet.'"

He drove back into Smithville as if on autopilot. The shadows had grown long. He glanced at the truck's clock. Ten minutes after eight. He wasn't particularly hungry, but he had a promise to keep. Before she died, Sally extracted several commitments from him, one being that he'd eat regular meals.

He brought the one-ton truck to rest in front of The Katy House then walked the two blocks to the restaurant. Patrons filled every seat at the bar, but there were several open tables. He put his back to a wall and placed his straw cowboy hat on an open chair. A male server sporting a beard and a man-bun delivered a menu and took his order for a glass of iced tea.

Laughter erupted from the bar then subsided like waves rolling to shore and slipping back out to sea. Fen scanned the crowd for potential trouble. The old habits of wearing a badge for twenty years were slow to die. Everyone here seemed to know each other. Heads turned to look at him. Shoulders shrugged as whispers behind cupped hands floated over the bar. A normal reaction to a stranger invading one of the local watering holes.

The delivery of his iced tea preceded him ordering a small pizza and a dinner salad. It seemed like a safe bet in this place where people at the bar outnumbered those sitting at tables by three to one.

Drinking tea gave him something to do besides checking his phone for messages that didn't exist. It also allowed him to look into the mirror behind the bar. One by one, he examined the faces and clothes of the stool sitters. Western-cut jeans and T-shirts were the uniform of the day for most of the men. The women wore a mixed bag of T-shirts, jeans, and off-the-rack dresses. The exception was a woman with raven hair flowing down her back. It surprised him when his eyes met hers in the mirror. He realized she was studying him with equal intensity.

She left her stool and took steps toward him. Her progress halted when her phone rang and she answered. He missed her name but caught enough words to determine her occupation.

She dropped the phone into her purse, and continued her short walk to his table. He stood.

"Hello, Sheriff Maguire. I'm Audrey West."

Fen held out a hand to an empty seat. "Please, counselor, join me."

She tilted her head in a way that said he'd surprised her by guessing she was an attorney. She recovered and flashed a bright smile while green eyes sparkled. He guessed her age at early-to-mid-forties, within a year or two of his but without the wear and tear.

Audrey wagged a finger. "You eavesdropped on my phone call. That's not fair. What else do you know about me?"

"You only confirmed what I suspected. The unwrinkled silk blouse told me you changed after work. Your jeans are designer and have a crease in them so sharp it could only mean you order extra starch from the dry cleaners. The boots are custom made. In a town this size I narrowed down your occupation to banker or attorney."

He took a breath and continued. "You're right about me not

playing fair. I've trained myself to listen to conversations. Bankers rarely discuss issues involving police jurisdiction. How'd I do?"

"As I expected." She then extended a delicate hand for him to shake. "Among other things, I'm the City Attorney for this booming metropolis. Part-time only. I understand you had a busy morning."

"I'd describe it as hot, sweaty, and, in all ways, unpleasant. It reminded me too much of the jobs I used to have."

"It's not every man who works ten years as a highway patrolman and another ten as a sheriff." She leaned forward. "How's the leg?"

It was Fen's turn to tilt his head in surprise. "You're well informed. You must have spoken with Ben Crump."

"Among others."

She didn't volunteer any other sources, so he moved on and answered her question about his leg. "If I wasn't such a stubborn fool, I'd have had the knee replaced many years ago. Nobody's asking me to play on their soccer team, but the physical therapy made a new man out of me."

Fen took a drink at the same time Audrey raised her glass and sipped. He couldn't help but chuckle.

"What's funny?"

"You're sitting close enough for me to smell wine, but that's not what's in your glass. The bartender must know to put water in it unless you specify wine. You came here to listen, not socialize."

The slightest of nods told him he'd discovered something else about her.

"You're partially correct. This bar is how I keep my finger on the pulse of Smithville. It's a gold mine of gossip."

"Only partially correct?"

"I came here to meet you and see what you thought about the homicide."

"Homicide? Are you sure?"

"The justice of the peace missed the stab wounds to the chest. He should have retired years ago. Left his glasses at home, so he didn't bother lifting the shirt. Ben Crump double-checked with the pathologist in Austin." Audrey ran a finger around the rim of her glass. "I'm interested in hearing what you think."

Fen didn't hesitate. "Until someone finds the original crime scene, this case will be a jurisdictional mess. The only real clue is the clothes the man was wearing. They might get lucky with DNA to identify him, but we can't assume at this point that an original sample exists."

"You're not very encouraging, but keep going."

"I got a good look at the underside of his hands. He'd been in the water too long to expect anything from fingerprints."

Fen summed up his thoughts. "Someone will eventually rise to the top and supervise the investigation, but don't be surprised if there's a turf fight."

Audrey puffed out her cheeks and released a breath. "There's so many things to get through before the investigation can begin in earnest. This will take a long time and cost the city, county, and state a lot of money."

Fen's salad arrived before his pizza. He looked into Audrey's green eyes and stammered, "Have you eaten?"

"Not yet."

The server asked, "Should I bring another salad?"

The words leaped from Fen's mouth without him thinking. "Bring it. How big is the pizza?"

"Big enough for two, as long as you're not starving."

"Bring two plates."

Audrey didn't object.

Chapter Four

Fen kept to his daily ritual of speaking to the photograph of his late wife, telling her details of yesterday's events. He began with the body in the river and ended with his dinner with Audrey. He kissed her photo and set it on the nightstand, ready to start his day. The morning was relatively cool for June and a walk sounded good. It wasn't his normal practice to pack tennis shoes on an overnight trip, but something told him to bring them this time. After retrieving them from his truck, he went to a rocking chair on the porch to put them on. An ambling stroll through the heart of the small city took him mostly north, past businesses, and into residential neighborhoods. It occurred to him that the vast majority of the houses, like the businesses, looked like they belonged in a black-and-white movie. Homes varied in size, from stately multi-story antebellum architecture, with wrap-around porches to modest two and three-bedroom dwellings. Many could stand a team of skilled craftsmen.

He pressed on until he spied the home that had captured Sally's heart. The *Hope Floats* house boasted the most impressive upper and lower semi-circle porches Fen had ever seen. In his mind's eye, he saw actors Sandra Bullock and Harry Connick, Jr., living happily ever after in this stately home.

Wanting to see more, he followed a gravel trail around the side of the house. A gate stood open, so he walked on, hoping he wasn't trespassing. From the street, he hadn't realized that the home sat on a high bank of the Colorado River. Its backyard was lush with freshly mowed grass. His attention turned to the lot next to it. The grass there was thigh-high, making the lot look like an abandoned stepchild.

Backtracking, he climbed the seldom-used road up and out of the riverbed and back into the neighborhood. It may have been a silly thing to do, but like so many visitors to Smithville, he used his phone to take pictures of the home. He'd show it to Sally that evening when he returned home to Newman County.

Cool air brought relief when Fen stepped back into The Katy House. His taste buds stood at attention when he entered the dining room. The long walk had done its job to fully activate his appetite.

The swinging door to the kitchen eased open and a woman appeared. She wore an apron and a broad smile. "There you are. I'm so sorry I didn't get to meet you yesterday. I try not to pry, but I absolutely love to get to know our guests."

"No problem," said Fen. "Your daughter did an excellent job of making me feel at home." Fen sniffed the air. "Are you responsible for those heavenly smells coming from the kitchen?"

"I wish I could take all the credit, but my husband is a professional chef. They're his recipes. Have a seat and I'll bring your juice. There's a carafe of fresh coffee."

Eloise proceeded to deliver a meal that lived up to all the

five-star reviews he'd read. The quality and quantity were truly overwhelming. She asked, "Can I get you anything else?"

Fen smiled and said, "I'd be an awfully ungrateful man if I asked for anything else. This is wonderful."

"Take your time. I'll be in the kitchen if you need anything."

Fen put a portion of the omelet that could easily feed two on his plate, added bacon and a biscuit, then smothered the biscuit with gravy.

As Fen laid his fork and knife across his plate, Eloise came out of the kitchen. Pleasantly stuffed, he said, "That had to be the best breakfast ever. The reviews on your website seemed too good to be true, but you surpassed them." He lowered his voice as if sharing a secret. "If anyone tells my cook I said that, I'll deny it."

The host gave him an exaggerated wink. "What's said at this table stays at the Katy House."

Fen topped off his cup of coffee as his hostess took a seat at the table. "Normally we have a full house of summer travelers. This is one of those strange nights where three people canceled for various reasons. We're fully booked tonight and reservations continue to flow in."

Fen made a snap decision. "What's the chances of me renting the room I'm in for the third week of September?"

"All week?"

He nodded. "I'm an artist. The Lost Pines Artisan's Guild is sponsoring a class I'll be teaching on painting landscapes."

The woman consulted the calendar on her phone and smiled. "You're in luck. The Texas Room is booked that week, but I have one room open. It's the Katy Tower, which is in a separate building overlooking the backyard."

"I'll take it as long as it comes with a repeat of this breakfast."

She made notes on her phone. "That's another week completely booked." The woman breathed a sigh. "People said we were fools for trying to keep this B&B open. My husband told me if we provided the best experience possible, it would be an excellent investment. He was right."

She glanced down at her coffee cup, then back at him. "I see you're wearing a wedding band. Will your wife be joining you in September?"

The kick to Fen's gut wasn't as hard as he expected. "I wish, but Sally died a few years ago. The ring simplifies my life."

"I'm so sorry." She spoke in a whisper. "Open mouth, insert foot."

"No need to apologize."

He needed to change the subject, so he spoke the first thing that came to his mind. "I took a long walk around town this morning."

She corrected him. "Not too long of a walk. The town isn't big enough for that. Did you go to the *Hope Floats* house and take pictures?"

He nodded an affirmative answer and smiled. "I guess that proves I'm an outsider."

"Everyone who visits has to have a photo. That movie isn't the only one filmed in Smithville, but it made the biggest splash."

Fen resettled in his chair. "I hope I wasn't trespassing, but I followed a gravel trail around the side of the house."

"You weren't trespassing. The gate is supposed to stay open because the riverfront lot next to the home is city property. There's been talk of making it into a park, but the city won't do it."

"Why not?"

"The reason I've heard is that they don't want to spend money on property in the floodplain. They have a point because the river gets out and covers it every few years." She took a breath. "Still, it wouldn't hurt to mow it. As it is, nobody uses it."

The conversation took a turn when she said, "Tell me if this is none of my business, but were you the out-of-towner who helped the police yesterday?"

Fen gave a single nod. "All I did was give advice on securing the area when a group of people pulled a body out of the river."

"That's not the story going around. People are saying you used to be a Texas Ranger, and you took charge until the police arrived."

Fen groaned. "It's amazing how fast stories veer from the truth. I used to be a state trooper and was the sheriff of Newman County. Now, I'm an artist, trying to mind my own business."

"I should have known there was more to the story than what's going around. Did they identify the victim?"

"Not as of last night. I ran into the city attorney at the restaurant you recommended."

The distance between her eyebrows narrowed. "I didn't recommend a restaurant."

Fen tilted his head. "What about the note left on this table? I have it in my room."

She chuckled. "That sounds like something Audrey would do. She's a sly one."

"What do you mean?"

"She knows to come in through the kitchen door during the day. My guess is she wanted to get another firsthand account of what happened, so she left a note for you to find. Was it signed?"

Fen thought hard. "Now that you mention it, no."

"Did the note recommend The Front Room, two blocks

from here?"

"Uh-huh."

"She goes there to pick up gossip."

Fen spoke before he thought, mainly because Audrey had outwitted him. "Is that all she picks up at the bar?"

This earned a boisterous laugh. "You can relax on that account. Audrey never married, but she adopted a son. He's the only man in her life."

Fen realized his lips had pursed together tight. Was he angry? No, but he was perplexed. He rose from the table and brought his emotions under control. "You have a lovely home, a breakfast that can't be beat, and I'm looking forward to coming back in September."

"I'm so glad you gave us a chance to serve you. Are you in a hurry to leave town?"

Fen's thoughts shot back to his home. "I have a young artist protegé named Bailey living over my garage who will have my scalp if I don't get home by early afternoon. We sell our paintings all over the state at various fairs and exhibits. This week's is in San Antonio. We'll load everything tonight and be on the road before dawn tomorrow."

It took him mere moments to pack his bag then say his goodbyes. One thing was for sure: he'd not mention a word of the alluring city attorney to either Bailey or Thelma. Those two would be impossible to live with if they so much as smelled the scent of another woman. What happened in Smithville, which was only a pleasant dinner, stayed in Smithville.

Overall, it had been a good trip and he looked forward to returning to paint various locations outside Smithville with his students. Passing the state park, he noticed there were some killer views, true vistas giving panoramic views of the distant verdant fields. Perhaps some of the students would want to paint them.

He wagged his head. "I may need to take the phrase *killer views* out of my vocabulary. Smithville probably hasn't logged a homicide in ten years. I show up, and here comes a body down the river."

His thoughts returned to yesterday morning. He glanced at the time on his truck's computer screen. It was twenty-four hours ago that trash pickers pulled the victim out of the river. "I wonder if Ben Crump found any additional evidence."

Fen's hand went up as a stop sign. "Don't go there. This isn't your case. I'm going home, pack this truck, and leave tomorrow morning to sell paintings with Bailey. End of Story."

The miles ticked by as he took in the rolling hills dotted with cattle, trees of various varieties, and small streams. The few towns he passed through were mostly of the size that had volunteer fire departments. At the one-hour point in his journey, another thought slipped into his mind. Audrey.

It occurred to Fen that he'd not told Sally everything about the time he'd spent talking to the city attorney. He quickly dismissed the omission as a pastoral scene to his right captured his attention.

The sun glinted off the windshield of a new tractor in the middle of a half-plowed field. He pulled over to the side of the road. Next to the fence sat the father of the new, massive tractor, standing proud and strong in the distance. The older tractor was still in service but looked worn and tired compared to the new metal beast. Fen climbed out of his truck and snapped photos of the two mechanical workhorses from various angles. He imagined a painting that showed two generations of the machines. "*Generations* would be a good name."

Satisfied he had a solid idea for his next painting, Fen climbed back into his truck and continued his journey home. He was looking forward to a good weekend selling his works with Bailey.

Chapter Five

As the diesel truck ate up the miles, he continued to mull over the possibilities of the painting. He pulled into the driveway of his home overlooking the four-thousand-acre ranch. Bailey came out to meet him. With hands on hips, she wasn't smiling. "What took you so long?"

Before he could grab his overnight bag, the nineteen-year-old turned on a heel and retreated into the house, slamming the door behind her. Fen followed her, wondering what had put her in such a foul mood. The front door flew open as he reached for the handle. In front of him stood Thelma, his housekeeper and cook, with hands tented on hips. "What took you so long?"

He wondered if a strain of sour dispositions and arms akimbo had hit his home. "That's the second time I've been asked that question since I arrived. What's with you and Bailey? I took some back roads from Smithville and stopped to take photos of a field that will be my next painting."

A downward gaze of contrition followed. "I'm sorry, Mr.

Fen, but that child stomped on my last frazzled nerve this morning. Combine that with my hot flashes and I'm not fit to be around."

She extended her hand and took his travel bag. "I hope you're not hungry. Bailey was ready to hit the trail two hours ago. She got an email from the folks in San Antonio saying y'all need to set up tonight. All you need to do is repack your bag with clean clothes. I've already laid them out on your bed."

Fen flipped his now empty hand to show the news didn't bother him. "We'll only be gone three nights. "

"Don't want you looking like a hobo in a rail yard."

"And I appreciate it."

As usual, Thelma seemed to climb down from the emotional precipice enough that he could ask a question and not receive a snippy response. "What's wrong with Bailey?"

Thelma didn't have to think. "Man troubles."

"Ah. That will do it. What's the latest crisis?"

"She got stood up for a date. That handsome deputy from Georgetown had to work overtime again."

Fen puffed out his cheeks and released a full breath of air. "Long distance romances rarely last. If it's meant to be, they'll work it out. The drive to San Antonio will do her good."

Thelma turned and spoke over her shoulder. "The mail and local newspaper are on the table where I always put them."

Nothing of interest awaited him in terms of mail so he picked up the latest bi-weekly edition of Springdale's newspaper and headed into the kitchen.

He'd only made it past the center fold when Thelma returned holding the shirt he'd worn the previous night. Her eyelids were narrow slits of accusation. "Smell the collar on this." She tossed the shirt at him.

He spoke before he sniffed it. "What am I supposed to

smell?" He then took in a whiff through his nose. "It's perfume."

Thelma's eyebrows raised. "It sure is."

Fen held up a hand to blunt the accusation. "Smithville's city attorney gave me a hug last night."

Bailey picked that moment to walk into the kitchen. Fen realized she'd heard what sounded like a confession when she said, "You picked up a woman at a bar last night?"

"No!"

Thelma took the shirt from Fen's hand and gave it to Bailey. "Smell this and tell me what you think."

Bailey did so and said, "Whoever she is, she uses expensive bait to catch her prey." Her earlier impatience with him forgotten, she sat in a chair and said, "Tell us about her."

"Do you want the whole story, or are you two happier when you jump to conclusions?"

The two women looked at each other. Bailey spoke for both of them. "The whole story, and don't leave out any of the juicy details."

"It all started yesterday morning when I was scouting places to paint. I was at a park, standing on a platform overlooking the Colorado River when a group of kayaks came down the river. One of them had a rope tied around a dead man and was pulling him to shore."

Fen wanted to allow the words to settle before he proceeded, but Bailey's response was immediate. "No way!"

Thelma corrected her. "Mr. Fen don't lie when it comes to bodies in rivers." She pulled out a chair. The two stared at him expectantly.

It was at least ten minutes before Fen completed his narrative. Bailey seemed to bristle with excitement. "Did you volunteer us to help with the investigation?"

"Of course not."

"Why not? You and me could have the case solved in less than a week."

"It's simple," said Fen. "We haven't been asked to help. If you don't remember, that's what they pay people with badges and guns to do."

Thelma chimed in. "You attract dead people like nobody I've ever met. Every time you leave Newman County you're trippin' over another body. Leave this one alone. I've got a bad feelin' about it."

Fen huffed. "Didn't you two hear me? Bailey and I have a full schedule of painting and shows lined up this summer through most of the fall. By the time we get to Smithville to teach the class in September, the killer will be in jail awaiting trial."

His optimism fell on deaf ears, but at least Thelma changed the conversation. "I want to know more about this attorney that set a trap for you and left her scent on the collar of your shirt. Describe her."

Fen shrugged. "If you two want to know more about her, drive to Smithville and knock on her door. I'm driving to San Antonio."

Thelma cut her gaze to Bailey. "I guess that's all we're gonna' get out of him." She stood and said, "You'd better have a sandwich before you leave. It's a long drive."

"I'm good," Fen said as he rose.

Her eyelids narrowed. "Why aren't you hungry?"

"I stuffed myself with a late breakfast. They serve it at nine o'clock."

"That's way too late," said Thelma. "Was it any good?"

The word "delicious" slipped out before he could stop it.

Thelma let out a loud harrumph. Fen tried to cover his tracks. "Of course, it wasn't as good as what you serve."

Bailey shook her head. "You've done it now. Thelma and I

looked up the Katy House online. They had photos of the rooms and the spread they put on for breakfast. How was the maple-infused bacon?"

Fen turned and walked out of the kitchen. "I'm packing and leaving before a cast iron skillet finds its way to the top of my head."

"That might be a good idea," said Thelma.

Fen shut the back door of his truck and saw Sam, his ranch manager and Thelma's husband, riding up on his lineback dun horse that stood fourteen hands high. He slipped out of the saddle with practiced efficiency, landing without making a sound. Fen expected nothing less from the full-blood Choctaw Indian and said, "Glad you showed up. I have a special assignment for you."

As usual, Sam showed no emotion. "I thought you might. Thelma called and told me about the body you found in the Colorado. She said someone dragged it in behind a kayak."

"I was there when they brought him to shore. There's a game warden that could use help in locating the original crime scene."

Sam shot back, "I don't work with cops."

"Then don't let anyone see you searching the riverbanks. He knows you're coming, and I told him you work alone."

Sam looked toward the sky. "There's a full moon tonight with clear skies." His gaze shifted back to Fen. "I can only cover about five miles."

"That's enough to search both banks. Go from bridge to bridge. You'll see them on your phone. There's thick brush that can conceal your truck by the Loop 230 public boat access."

Sam had all the information he needed. He grabbed the saddle horn, jumped, and pulled himself into the saddle. His feet found the stirrups as if they were radar-guided. "I'll call you tomorrow morning and let you know if I found anything."

The clip-clops of Sam's horse were fading when Bailey peeked from around the back of the truck. "You're a sneaky man."

Fen shrugged. "The game warden is an old friend who's near retirement. He deserves a helping hand and a quick solution to the murder."

Bailey stuck out her bottom lip. "That may be, but it blows our chance to work on an interesting murder."

"In case you forgot, we're artists and there's a show to work that starts tomorrow afternoon."

Bailey gave him a hard stare. "The only things left to pack are the brushes, paints, and advertising materials."

"I guess we should get to it then."

With goodbyes said and a cooler of drinks and snacks in the backseat, Fen pointed the loaded diesel toward the gate. After driving almost an hour in silence, he turned to Bailey. "There's something I want to show you. It's not far."

"What is it?"

"My next painting." He pulled out his phone and handed it to her. "Look at the pictures I took this morning and tell me what you think."

She manipulated his phone and pushed her eyebrows together. "Tractors? Why do you want to paint tractors?"

"They're telling a story."

"They are?"

"Sure. The old generation is giving way to the next one. It's younger, stronger, and bolder. Notice how big the plowed field is, and how tired the older tractor looks."

"I see what you're saying, but the proportions are wrong. The tractors will be tiny."

"I'll move them to the foreground, so the story will make sense. Artistic license."

Bailey wrinkled her nose. "That works for you, but I'm a

realist. I'd rather paint a close-up of the old and forget about the one that looks too new and shiny.

Fen shook his head. "Do that and you lose the broadness of time and the multiplicity of things the work could speak to people."

Bailey enlarged the photo which cropped the sides, top, and bottom. She announced, "That's better. I still say only one thing at a time."

It didn't surprise him that they didn't come to an agreement. It was a game they played. He'd stake out a position and she'd challenge him on it. Sometimes the subject dealt with painting, sometimes it was what to eat, and more often than not, it was if she was going to pursue a degree in art. The one topic they agreed to never discuss was politics. For that, he was thankful.

He pulled off the road and pointed when they came to a stop. "See what I mean about the scope? Imagine putting that shiny, new tractor in the foreground with the old one off to the side."

Bailey looked into the field. "It would work better if you offset the new tractor from the middle and had the old one only half on the canvas. That would symbolize its replacement and eventual passing away."

Fen nodded. "You're right."

She jerked her head and stared at him. "What did you say?"

"I said you're right. It would show the passing of the baton from one generation to the next."

Bailey grinned. "I'm not completely right. You nailed it by representing time with the field. I can see the plowed furrows disappearing over a hill." She looked at what she'd described. "Life keeps going no matter what."

Fen said, "Even when a boyfriend disappoints you?"

"I feel a lecture coming on."

"Not today. There are some things you need to discover on your own."

Chapter Six

It was a normal, mid-September day as Fen sat in his studio considering the trip back to Smithville. Twenty-five participants had registered for the five-day class that was light on instruction and heavy on painting. His plan was to give a two-hour lecture on Monday morning, then show enlarged photos of the various sites he'd selected. The participants could choose whether they wanted to paint a long, narrow river scene of the Colorado, two lake scenes, or a panorama of mostly open fields with a thick pine forest in the distance. Once they decided, they'd travel to the location of their choice and spend the rest of the day completing sketches and taking photos. His job was to check on each student's progress and give them pointers on getting started.

On Tuesday, the students would meet together briefly at a studio in town with completed sketches which he would critique. The rest of the day, and the week, would involve him bouncing between the various locations, offering encouragement. Saturday, they'd display their work at a public art show.

Those who desired could set up booths at the park by the railroad museum and try to entice buyers to purchase whatever works they brought.

His phone came to life, jolting him out of his mental trip to the small town on the Colorado River. Fen groaned when he saw the name of his friend and personal attorney, Chuck Forsythe. The lawyer and his wife Candy were two of his best friends and had been for years. They saw him through Sally's illness and death. Fen credited the couple with keeping him from going off the rails.

The reason for his groan was that a phone call from Chuck wasn't always social. It could also mean they wanted him to drop everything and investigate a murder. He answered with unease in his voice. "Good morning, Chuck."

"Long time, no see. Can you stop by the office today?"

A wave of suspicion crashed over Fen. "Business or pleasure?"

"Both. Candy has fresh scones waiting for you."

"This has to be serious. Do you remember that I'm booked next week? That means I'm packing for painting and nothing else. I can't get out of it, so don't ask."

Chuck answered with a laugh. "I didn't forget, and you'll leave for Smithville and stay the week doing your art thing."

"As long as you understand that, I'll be by this morning."

"Candy has your coffee mug relatively clean and ready to fill."

That bit of information put a quick end to the call. Candy's homemade scones were a treat he couldn't resist. Fen looked at his phone before slipping it into his pocket. "Chuck's up to something."

The knock on the door prompted him to put aside thoughts of what Chuck and Candy wanted. "Come in," he shouted.

Bailey spoke as she approached. "Are you planning out the trip to Smithville?"

"Yep."

"Who were you talking to?"

"Chuck."

Her eyes widened. "Are we going to see him? Is it another murder? Where's this one?"

"You're rounding third base and I haven't stepped into the batter's box." He sucked in a breath. "Whatever he wants to talk about, we're not available until after we return from Smithville. I've committed to a week of teaching. You and Ren will paint all week and sell as much as you can on Saturday."

"It's such a bummer she and I don't get to stay at the bed and breakfast."

"Don't blame me. Only one room was available."

Pouting and frustration flavored Bailey's next words. "Cory and I broke up for all of two days. How was I to know we'd get back together so soon?"

She looked at the sketch Fen had completed of the two tractors. "It's good, but I still don't think it tells much of a story."

"You may be right. That's why I'm taking it with me to work on."

Fen put his pencil away and asked, "How many works are you taking?"

"Six that I'm happy with and four more to get rid of. Six portraits, two wildlife pencil drawings, and two landscapes. Ren and I will take turns drawing caricatures to make sure there's cash flow if sales are slow. She'll also try to get commissions to do murals on buildings."

This was the first time Bailey's friend, Ren, would be working a full show with them. He had taught her to do caricatures, but her real talent lay in painting large scale building murals. Fen stood. "Ren has a genuine talent for blending history into art. That takes research, skill, and time." Fen picked up his straw cowboy hat but didn't put it on. "You're still focused on portraits, which may be a good business decision. People love to look at themselves."

"As long as vanity exists, I'll make a decent living."

"Spoken like a true business woman. Give the people what they want." He took a step toward the door and stopped. "Make sure you pack for a full week. That hotel in Bastrop you and Ren are staying in doesn't have washers and dryers."

A sparkle came into her eyes. "I thought about asking Thelma to come see you at the B&B. Ren and I could drop off our dirty clothes halfway through the week. You could add yours to ours and Thelma could wash them."

Fen gave her an icy gaze. "Your idea of humor isn't working. I'd rather recommend someone sit on the couch between you and Cory the next time he comes to see you. Thelma seems like the logical choice."

Bailey's head took on the appearance of a metronome. "I'll pack enough for a week and an extra day or two."

"Excellent decision. Don't tell Thelma where I'm going this morning unless you want to answer a hundred questions neither of us has answers to."

Fen somehow slipped out of the house without Thelma stopping him. Perhaps she knew but was busy on the phone conducting her idea of business—collecting gossip. He painted and solved crimes. Thelma gathered rumors like Google mines data.

The trip into Springdale, the county seat, gave Fen about fifteen minutes to guess what kind of mission Chuck and Candy had for him. More than that, he wondered about the people who notified the attorney and his wife that they wanted him to look into wrongdoings, usually murder. He had no idea of their identity because they stayed in the shadows. All he'd been able to discern was they had significant influence throughout the state. Candy had made it clear that it would behoove him not to ask questions.

He trusted Chuck and Candy, but he had several rules he laid down before agreeing to give law enforcement a helping hand. The first was he worked *with* the police, not for them. This meant he ran his investigations with results, not policy manuals, in mind. Carrying a firearm was optional and totally up to him. This allowed him to get into certain places and situations that the police couldn't, or wouldn't. Lastly, he had full discretion in choosing others to help him as the situation demanded. Lou Cooper, a scrappy newspaper reporter, and Bailey had been instrumental in several of his investigations.

He pulled into a parking space at the rear of Chuck's law practice and thought about the most compelling reason for him to take part in another semi-clandestine murder investigation. "Here I go again, Sally. You made me promise that I'd not become a hermit stuck in my studio all day. I'm keeping my promise to you."

Fen entered the building and Candy shifted her gaze from a computer screen to the door. A nod and smile preceded her instruction. "Go back to Chuck's office. I'll bring your coffee and a scone."

"You sure know how to get me here in a hurry."

Chuck's spacious office sat at the end of a hallway. Fen entered without knocking. As usual, stacks of files littered his massive desk. He crossed the expanse, and settled in a chair opposite the attorney. "I thought you agreed to let Candy file some of that mess."

Chuck issued a dismissive glance. "I did, but I put an addendum on the promise. Files leave my desk only after the client is dead. She cleared off twenty-seven, and I'm busy replacing them."

Candy came in with a scone atop a small paper plate in one hand and a mug of coffee in the other. "He's hopeless." She pushed a pile of files back toward her husband and set the plate and coffee on the edge in front of Fen. A tower wobbled, but didn't fall.

Three minutes of small talk about harvesting crops and the price of cattle passed before Chuck nibbled around the edges of the real purpose of Fen being there. "What's the latest you've heard about the murder in Smithville?"

"Ben Crump stopped calling me with updates after Smithville's chief arrested Riley Eastham. It was his knife they found in the overgrown lot on the riverbank."

Chuck nodded. "The city-owned lot is definitely the site of the murder, and the lockblade knife they found there is the murder weapon." He leaned forward and folded his hands on the only clear spot on his desk. "Further investigation has revealed that Riley Eastham was in Dallas when the coroner determined the murder took place."

"Are they sure?"

"Hotel receipts and eyewitnesses."

Fen realized something wasn't adding up. "It's been almost three months. What took them so long to realize Riley couldn't have committed the crime?"

"It's a mess. Jurisdiction fell to the city once they established the original crime scene. They had the murder weapon, and Riley conveniently discovered the body. They assumed he orchestrated everything when he refused to answer questions."

Fen took a sip of coffee and resettled his mug on Chuck's desk. "It's not that unusual for someone to report a crime they committed. They believe it will help shift suspicion away from themselves."

"Right," said Chuck. "Riley's a smart and determined busi-nessman. As soon as the local cops hit him with a pointed question, he demanded an attorney. The knife gave the cops probable cause to arrest him. Fast forward two months and the grand jury returned a formal indictment. The DA prepared for trial, and the press had a juicy story to report."

More pieces fell into place in Fen's mind. "Let me guess. Riley's lawyer hired a private investigator who did a thorough job. He waited until damage was done to his client's reputation before revealing he had an airtight alibi. I smell a lawsuit against the city of Smithville."

"Exactly," said Candy. "A city that size has a hard enough time maintaining necessary services and keeping potholes in the streets filled. Now, there's a lot of hand-wringing and finger-pointing among the local officials and concerned citizens."

Fen used his imagination to picture the town's council meetings. "What they're really afraid of is a jury awarding Riley Eastham a fat settlement. People get touchy when politicians throw words around like tax increases."

Chuck took a thick file from the top of the stack nearest him, stood, and extended it over the desk. "These are copies of reports from all the agencies that investigated the murder. There's also a report from the coroner."

A wave of trepidation washed over Fen as he took possession of the confidential information. "I hope you remember I won't be able to start on this until after next week."

"Why not? You're going to Smithville Sunday afternoon." Unsullied innocence filled Chuck's words. "I know why you're going, and it will make a perfect cover for you, Bailey, and Lou. If you remember our conversation earlier this morning, I promised that you'd do your art thing. That still leaves early mornings, evenings, and nights to find the person or persons who killed Lee Grimes."

Candy spoke before Fen could defend himself. "It would

also be nice if you could help the city get out of the trouble they find themselves in. We understand you've already met the city attorney. From what I hear, she's a very interesting woman." She smiled in a motherly way. "Eat your scone. They always put you in a better mood."

Chapter Seven

Fen mumbled as he drove back to his ranch. He should have known Chuck and Candy's priorities didn't line up with his. They ranked a murder and lawsuit against a small town higher than his commitment to teach. It didn't matter that he'd made his promise nine months ago.

Fen snorted through his nose as if that would help relieve his foul mood. He spoke out loud, even though no one was there to hear his words. "What really burns my biscuits is Chuck knows I'll now be thinking more about the murder than teaching art. He counted on it when he ambushed me." He took a breath. "Yeah, that's what he did. He ambushed me, just like someone ambushed the victim, Lee Grimes."

He then played mental tennis with himself. "How do you know it was an ambush? You haven't read the crime scene reports or the autopsy report." He sighed. "Perhaps not, but someone stabbed him in the chest. At least Ben Crump had sense enough to call the coroner.

"So," said Fen to himself, as he crossed the bridge spanning the Brazos River. "Someone hated the victim enough to stab him up close and personal, then dump him in the river."

Fen seldom talked to himself out loud, but this seemed like a good time to do it. "That's true. It's also true that Chuck and Candy don't call me until the locals have either run out of clues or find themselves in a real bind."

He turned off the highway. "Are Chuck and Candy hiding something from me?

"It's possible." Fen let out a chuckle. "No, it's not only possible, it's likely. I'm not sure I liked the little smile on Candy's face when she said Audrey West was a very interesting woman. I smell long-distance matchmaking. No thanks."

He held up four fingers on his left hand as he said, "I have four things I'm going to do in Smithville—just four. I'm going to teach the class during the day and finish my painting of the tractors in the evening. That's two. Next, I'll do what I can to solve a murder. If there's any time left, I'll see what I can do to help the City of Smithville avoid a lawsuit. Candy must be out of her mind if she thinks I'll have time to look twice at a woman; I don't care how green her eyes are."

Fen finished his lecture to himself and turned off the main road onto a county road. The rest of his trip home went without words, but his gaze shifted several times to the file sitting on the seat next to him. Like an unexpected present wrapped in shiny paper with a nice bow, it seemed to dare him to open it.

After parking in the garage, he grabbed the folder and hustled inside. Thelma caught him as he walked through the back door. She took one look at the brown folder and narrowed her eyes. "That lawyer friend of yours is up to no good. I knew it the minute I saw you sneak out of here. I hope you told him you weren't available until after you get back from Smithville then rest a full week."

Fen didn't need to ask how she knew where he went. She

could extract more information from what he called her *network of spies* than any detective he'd ever met.

"I told him painting was priority number one."

He then mentally spoke a word of thanksgiving when his phone rang, saving him from Thelma's inevitable barrage of follow-up questions. She huffed in disgust, spun on one heel, and walked away as he allowed the phone to ring several times before saying, "Hello."

The caller spoke as he closed the door to his studio behind him. "Mr. Maguire, this is Eloise with The Katy House Bed and Breakfast."

"Hello, Eloise. What can I do for you?"

"I hate being the bearer of bad news, but I took a nasty fall going down the back steps. I have one broken arm and severely strained ligaments in my left ankle. The doctor has me on bed rest for ten days. I'm calling to tell you how sorry I am for having to cancel your reservation. You'll receive a full refund."

Disappointment sometimes has a taste of its own. This was one of those times. It reminded him of a time when he was ten years old. With a super-sour jawbreaker in his mouth, he stood by his father's truck. Camping gear and fishing poles lay in the truck's bed. His dad exited through the front door of their home wearing a scowl instead of his normal smile.

"Bad news, son. Grandpa had a heart attack and may not make it. I need you to unload everything in the truck while I go to the hospital in the car."

Fen realized he'd not responded to Eloise as she kept talking. "I can't apologize enough for inconveniencing you. It isn't often that we get someone staying a full week, and I was so looking forward to seeing some of your paintings."

The super-sour taste of the invisible jawbreaker made him want to brush his teeth. His brain, however, kicked into gear and told him to delay. This was something that he'd trained himself to do when hit with unexpected bad news. The words shot forth as if someone else was speaking. "Have you canceled my reservation?"

Eloise hesitated. "Not yet. I canceled the others. You're the last on my list."

"Good. Please call me back before you do anything about mine." Another thought came to him. "I forgot how many rooms you have."

"There's six, three in the main house and three more in separate buildings in the backyard. I don't understand how that can help. My husband has an international trip he can't get out of. He's helping to open a new restaurant in Portugal. Our daughter will be my nurse, so she can't even welcome guests."

"I understand," said Fen as his mind worked at double four-four time. "Give me at least twenty minutes. Not all my ideas are good, but I think this one might be."

Eloise hesitated, but not for long. "I'll take no action on your reservation until after I call you back."

"Thanks, and I'm so sorry about your arm and ankle."

"It was my fault for being in such a hurry. I can't imagine what you're up to, but you're a good man. That much, I'm sure of. I'll call you back."

Fen sent a text to Bailey, who was likely painting in her studio/efficiency apartment over the garage. He then left his studio in search of Thelma. He found her in the kitchen, extracting potatoes and carrots from the refrigerator. She placed the items on the counter and turned to face him. "You cheated me out of giving you a lecture about that lawyer."

"Save it for later. I need to talk to you and Bailey in the living room."

Thelma's eyebrows shot up. "Living room talks are for serious matters. Something big is up."

"Big enough." He turned and walked out of the kitchen.

Bailey arrived a short time after he settled in a recliner. Thelma sat at the far end of the brown leather couch, while the other artist-in-residence took her place nearest him and asked, "What's up?"

"That's what I want to know," said Thelma. "It isn't every day we have a family meeting so to speak."

Fen cast a sly grin toward Thelma. "How would you like to come to Smithville to take care of Bailey, Ren, Lou, and me?"

Thelma's response came without a beat of hesitation. "Did lawyer Chuck give you some of his moonshine nobody's supposed to know about? You never want me to go out of town with you. The last three times I tried to cook and clean for you, I felt your boot on my backside."

Fen ignored the complaint, even though there was truth in it. "This time is different. The owner of the B&B had an accident, and the doctor has her in bed for ten days. Her husband can't get out of a commitment to go to Portugal. She's canceled all reservations except mine." His gaze fixed on Thelma. "I want you to come to Smithville with us."

Thelma tilted her head. "I know you, Fen Maguire. That isn't all the story."

Fen held up empty hands. "Cooking and cleaning is all I want you to do. It's a beautiful old home with a kitchen designed by a professional chef."

"How many bedrooms?"

"Six, but we'll only use five."

Thelma brought her chin up. "I never was very good at math, but there's only the three of us plus Lou. Who else do you plan on inviting?"

Bailey took over. "I'll need to cancel hotel reservations for me and Ren if we're staying with you. Add Ren and it makes five."

Bailey and Thelma traded looks. Bailey's quick mind put the pieces together. "They never solved the murder case."

Thelma let out a whoop. "That explains why you went to see Chuck and Candy this morning. I knew they were up to something."

Fen needed to tap the brakes on their enthusiasm. "Bailey, I want you to understand that my primary focus next week is teaching and painting. I'll be busy doing that from nine in the morning until five in the afternoon. Chuck gave me a file folder containing reports that various agencies and departments have already completed. Lou will do research and add to the file. If the names of any teens or young adults rise to the surface, I may ask you and Ren to befriend them and gather whatever information you can."

"Cool. Didn't you tell me the cop that was first on the scene when you found the body was sort of young?"

"Yeah. I already have him on my list of people for you to talk to. I doubt he'll be of much help, but you never know."

Fen noticed that Thelma had become uncharacteristically quiet. She'd suspected him of something clandestine. Now it was his turn to suspect her. Before he could inquire further, she rose from the couch and said, "Now that you've thrown a monkey wrench into my plans, there's a week's worth of work for me to do and only two days to do it in. Don't be surprised if you get sandwiches for supper."

Fen's raised hand became a stop sign. "Neither of you does anything until I hear from Eloise. She may turn down my offer to keep her B&B full next week."

Bailey rose to her feet as she and Thelma spoke over each other as they walked out of the room. Their excited babble included something to the effect that Eloise would surrender to Fen's charm and power of persuasion.

Fen went back to his studio. He didn't have long to wait until his phone rang. "Fen? This is Eloise."

"Thanks for calling me back." He didn't wait for her to respond. "I have a proposition for you. Now that your calendar is clear, I'd like to book all six of your rooms for next week even though only five of us will be there. Thelma is my cook, cleaner, and all-around helper with anything that takes place within the walls of my home. She'll do all the cooking and cleaning. There are two young-adult artists and a woman newspaper reporter named Lou Cooper, who'll also come. I'll vouch for everyone."

She said nothing for several seconds. "I'm taking powerful painkillers, so let me make sure I understand what you're proposing. You want to take all the rooms for an entire week, even though only five will be occupied."

"That's correct."

"And you're bringing your own woman to cook and clean?"

"She lives in a cottage behind my house and does it for me every day."

"This is highly unusual. My staff or I have always been on site when we've had guests. Then there's the liability issue." Her voice trailed off.

"Name your price on a deposit." Fen waited in the silence.

"I don't know. Let me talk with my husband first and I'll call you back."

"Sure. I understand. I'll be waiting to hear from you." Fen ended the call then walked over to the window. The pastures were taking on the late-summer hue of green mixed with pale yellow as the temps had been over one hundred the last couple of weeks.

He returned to his favorite chair and tried to relax. He hoped Eloise's husband could see the value of a week's worth of income as greater than any risk. If not, he and his crew would be stuck in a hotel twenty minutes from Smithville. Not the ideal situation given the multiple assignments for the week.

The phone rang fifteen minutes later, rousing him from reading reports in the file. "Hello."

"This is Eloise. My husband and I have decided to allow you to rent the rooms you need with one caveat—you'll only pay for five rooms."

"You don't have to do that," said Fen. "Believe me, you'll be doing me a huge favor by not making me stay in a hotel in Bastrop."

"Don't argue with me, Mr. Maguire. I can't charge you for an unoccupied room."

Fen asked, "Can you assure me you won't rent the last room to someone else?"

"Of course."

"Then we almost have a deal. I'll be responsible for all the food. What do you say?"

This time, she didn't hesitate. "I say you're an answer to our prayers. The house and all the rooms are yours."

After thanking her for being flexible, Fen hung up. There remained only one thing left to do, and that was to call Lou. The flashing text notification told him there was no need. A text had come in while he was on the call with Eloise.

Candy told me to call you this evening. I couldn't wait.
On my way to your ranch. Put a leash on you-know-who.

Fen smiled at his phone. Thelma and Lou had an on-again, off-again relationship. This must be their week of being off. A week in Smithville, living in the same house, might be good for both of them. If nothing else, it would be interesting.

Chapter Eight

Sunday morning went by in the usual way until Lou arrived fifteen minutes early. It was straight up eleven o'clock when the four of them found seats in the living room. Fen cleared his throat. "Let's get started. Ren will meet us in Smithville."

Bailey shook her head. "She stayed up way too late last night painting. At least, that's what she told me. Knowing her, she could have been painting their dog's nails."

Lou chimed in. "As scatterbrained as she is, there's no telling who or what she painted last night."

Fen took over before Thelma could give her opinion. "I made it clear to Eloise that I know and trust everyone staying at the B&B. She's doing us a huge favor by turning over her house to me for a full week."

Thelma looked like she wanted to throw in an opinion or two, but pressed her lips together.

Fen determined the meeting was off to a good start and kept going. "As far as anyone knows, Bailey, Ren, and I are in

Smithville to paint, and not to investigate a murder. Thelma is with us to cook and clean because Eloise is stuck in bed. That leaves Lou to invent a cover story that explains her presence with us."

"I already have," said Lou. "If asked, I'll say I booked a week at the Katy House to explore stories about the growth of Bastrop County. That will explain my going to the county courthouse to search official records. Also, I'll hit the public libraries in Bastrop and Smithville for unique historical documents. Sometimes, there are real treasures in small libraries."

Bailey asked, "What will you tell them if they ask why Eloise didn't cancel your reservation like she did the other guests?"

"That's simple," said Lou. "Tell them I threatened to sue her."

Fen nodded his approval. "Mine is that I made a special deal to rent out the rest of the B&B with the stipulation I'd bring my personal chef. Eloise couldn't turn down the money."

Thelma rubbed her hands together. "Eloise sounds like my kind of woman. I knew this was going to be a trip to remember. My horoscope told me."

Fen ignored the comment. "Thelma, tell me you're keeping the promise you gave me about not taking all your pots, pans, or anything else you normally cook with."

"I crossed my heart, didn't I?" Thelma then mumbled, "Don't blame me if nothing tastes the way it should. I'm not sure I can make gravy in anything but my old cast iron skillet."

"Is everyone packed for the week?" asked Fen.

Heads nodded.

"Good. Lou got a good jump on background checks. Do you want to go over suspects and persons of interest now or wait until we get to Smithville?"

"Let's hit the road," said Bailey. "You never know about Ren. She may wake up, down a double-shot espresso, follow it with an energy drink and beat us there."

"I'm raring to go," said Thelma.

Lou said, "I forgot my makeup bag and need to drive back into town and get it."

Fen closed the short meeting by saying, "Lou, Thelma, and I are staying in the main house. There's three rooms to choose from. Bailey and Ren are in separate buildings that overlook the backyard." He took a breath. "Let's go to Smithville. After everyone arrives and we're settled, we'll meet in the living room and I'll go over what I expect each of us to do this week."

FEN EASED his truck to a stop in front of The Katy House which sat on the corner of Ramona and 2nd Street. Thelma parked behind him. He motioned Bailey to pull up to where he stood in the street. Her window came down and he pointed as he gave instructions. "Go around the corner. You'll see two outbuildings overlooking the backyard. Take your pick of the three rooms; two are upstairs and one on ground level. I'll go inside and unlock the back door of the main house for you."

He retreated to his truck and pulled a suitcase and a travel bag from the back seat. Thelma followed him inside, but only brought one suitcase on her first trip. She spoke as she sat it on the floor and looked around. "This is a nice old house. It looks just like the pictures on their website. If it's all the same with you, I'd like the bedroom at the back of the house, the Bluebonnet room."

Fen's lip quirked. "I thought you would."

"Why's that?"

"Old houses tend to creak and squeak. I'll be in the Texas Special bedroom overlooking the front and Lou will be in the Katy Limited that's in the middle of the hall, so you'll be able to keep track of both of us. The bathroom of the Bluebonnet room has a view of the backyard which will help you keep tabs on Bailey and Ren."

Thelma tented her hands on her ample hips. "You don't know me as well as you think you do. I chose that bedroom because of the pretty bluebonnets painted on the clawfoot tub."

Fen chuckled. "Whatever you say, Thelma."

"In that case, I'm going to look at the kitchen."

Fen gave her a hard stare. "You won't need to buy anything for the kitchen but food. A trained chef equipped that kitchen, so I'm sure there's nothing you need to add to it. But if I were a betting man, I'd bet you ignored what I told you. You can't leave town without slipping that cast iron skillet in your truck. What else did you bring?"

Her sheepish expression told him he'd guessed right again. She squared her shoulders and raised a defiant chin. "I'll be the judge if this home has a proper kitchen or not. You run along and catch bad guys, or paint, or do whatever else you do when no one's looking."

It was nothing new for them to thrust and parry verbally. In fact, Thelma took great joy in the kitchen table sport of defending indefensible positions. He found her to be a worthy opponent. Sometimes she'd get the better of him.

He made a quick side trip to the kitchen, unlocked the back door, and stepped onto the small back porch. He glanced at the steps leading down to the sidewalk. This was where Eloise said she fell. Perhaps it was raining, or, she was in too big of a hurry, or she was carrying an awkward load. He hadn't asked her for an explanation, and she hadn't said. Not knowing sparked his curiosity and reminded him to focus on details. It also showed him he was rusty at gathering information.

Back inside, Thelma made a clockwise inspection of the kitchen. She reminded him of a military drill instructor looking for a loose thread on a soldier's uniform. Grunts and groans of displeasure provided part of the soundtrack of her slow, methodical search. "It ain't the way I'd arrange things. It'll take me all week to find what I need."

Fen escaped the domain she'd soon call her own and went back to his truck. Blaring rock music caught his attention before he recognized the rattles and wheezes of Ren's geriatric panel van. She brought it to a gasping stop behind Thelma's half-ton truck.

In a move that didn't surprise him, she piled out of the van, moved to the sidewalk, took a long look at the house, and did a cartwheel in the front yard. "What a gnarly old house! I wonder how many people have painted portraits of this regal grandma?"

"I bet quite a few," said Fen as he once again took the time to appreciate the craftsmanship. He was still examining the home when Ren took quick steps and enveloped him in a two-armed hug. The twenty-year-old broke the clench as fast as she'd given it. "Where's Bailey?"

"Around the corner. Park behind her, and you can put your things in your room. There's two to choose from."

"My own room? That's super awesome. This is much better than us sharing a hotel room in Bastrop." Her eyebrows wrinkled. "Don't get me wrong. I love Bailey like she's the sister I never had, but to stay in a real B&B and have a room to myself is like heaven. I can put in my noise-canceling earbuds, dance and paint, and not bother anyone."

Ren took a step toward her van and stopped with her foot still in the air. It was as if she were a bird dog catching the scent of a quail. Her gaze fixed on the wall of a building across the street. "You've got to be kidding me! There's a mural painted on that wall." She lowered her foot to the ground and took another tentative step forward. "It's a shame she's all faded. I wonder if they'd let me bring it back to life."

"You could ask."

A smile threatened to stretch her face. "Do you mean it? Really? You don't mind?"

"Not everyone is cut out to paint landscapes. You paint murals that bring history to life, and you're very good at it. Play to your strengths."

"You're the best, Fen."

"Go find Bailey. We'll have a short meeting after everyone gets settled."

The absence of crunching metal signaled Ren made the brief trip unscathed. He didn't make it back inside before Lou's Toyota Camry rounded the corner. Everyone was present and accounted for.

Lou was no stranger to travel. With over twenty-five years as a newspaper reporter, she'd covered stories all over the state and a few abroad. She packed light with clothes that didn't draw attention to herself. Everything coordinated, but didn't stand out. Her words of greeting revealed her personality. "I can't believe I've never been to Smithville before. It doesn't look like I missed much by not coming sooner."

"There's a river and a murder to solve. What more could you ask from a small town?" He looked at her lone suitcase. "Would you like me to take your bag upstairs?"

"Not on your life. The last time I let a man carry my luggage it ended in divorce number three. After that train wreck, I swore I'd carry my own bags." She quirked a smile. "Besides, it's not that heavy."

Bailey and Ren had claimed the couch when Fen came

inside. He gave Lou directions to her room and settled in an armchair to wait for her return. The squeaking stairs announced Lou's arrival as she made her way downstairs, and he rose from his chair. "I changed my mind. Let's meet in the dining room."

Chapter Nine

Fen stood at the head of the table and wasted no time in getting started. "This investigation is unlike any the three of us have done before. To begin with, Bailey and I won't be available from nine in the morning until at least four-thirty in the afternoon. Don't call us unless it's an emergency. That goes for Ren, too. Tomorrow morning she'll offer her skills to the business across the street. There's a mural on the outside wall that's faded. If they agree, she'll make it look new again."

"Darn right," said Ren.

Fen cast her a serious look. "You'll also keep your eyes and ears open. People will be curious about you repainting the mural. Get to know as many people as you can, but don't mention anything about the murder until the second or third time you talk to them."

"What if it comes up in conversation?"

"Act like this is the first you've heard of it."

"That won't be hard. I make friends easily and can talk about practically anything."

Fen shifted his gaze. "Thelma, I don't need to tell you how

to find out what's going on in a small town, but don't pressure people into talking. Your primary job is cooking and cleaning. You're also to get a feel for the town's history."

Thelma lifted her chin. "I know what you want. It's who done who wrong, and all that goes with it."

Fen didn't dispute her, but added, "Past *and* present. You'll probably need to get out and about until you develop sources."

Thelma huffed. "Next, you'll be telling me how to make gravy. I'll be in the grocery store this afternoon and come home with more than what I plan to cook."

Lou cast her gaze to him. "You've saved me for last. That doesn't bode well."

"It's your standard assignment, with one exception. The file you received from Chuck and Candy is thick, but almost all of it relates to the arrest and prosecution of Riley Eastham. Later this week, I need you to go to Dallas and verify his alibi. I also need thorough background checks on others whose names appear in the file. Start with the other trash pickers. We'll add people to your list as the week goes on."

He shifted his gaze to the other three. "Send Lou and me emails or texts when you come across something or someone's name you think might help the investigation. Don't wait until the end of the day."

Lou's gaze shifted to the coffeemaker. "You'd better make sure there's a full supply of those plastic pods of coffee. I have a feeling this investigation will take gallons." She then mumbled what was really on her mind. "There better be a great story that comes out of the work you want me to do."

"I think there'll be something you can use. Small towns have a lot of secrets. Let's hope a week is all it takes. Bailey and I have a fall festival in Conroe next week."

He took in a deep breath. "Bailey and Ren, there's a coffee shop three blocks east of here that opens at 6:00 a.m. Go there and hang out until eight in the morning, then come back here for breakfast."

"What about you?" asked Bailey.

"There's a bakery only a block away that has seating. I'll start my day there and try to find people who like to talk."

Thelma's head jerked up. "I know how you act when you go to a bakery. That belly of yours is already putting a strain on your belt."

Fen ignored the comment and looked at Lou. "You're included in the morning breakfast meetings at eight."

Lou gave her head a nod. "What about tonight?"

"You, Thelma, and I will split up. I'll go back to The Front Room Wine Bar. It has good food and plenty of conversations to eavesdrop on."

Thelma let her feelings be known when she let out a harrumph. "If there's a certain Jezebel wearing expensive perfume there, you better find another place to eat."

Lou raised her eyebrows but didn't pursue the subject further. "Going to a bar is a good idea. There's a beer garden right down the street. I'll go there and see if I can talk a lonely cowboy into buying me something cold and wet."

Fen looked at Thelma. "I need you to be flexible this week. "Some, or all of us, will miss meals if we have a lead to chase down. We'll need sack lunches every day unless we tell you otherwise."

Thelma threw up her hands, stood, and stomped her way back into the kitchen, mumbling as she went. "If I had a dollar for every meal I cooked for you that you didn't come home and eat, I'd be a wealthy woman."

Fen pulled a hand down his face. Thelma took great pride in her cooking. After all, she promised Sally that he'd eat a balanced diet and that pastries would be a treat. She was the self-imposed guardian of his health. Tomorrow morning he'd go to the bakery, limit himself to one pastry, stay two hours, and come back so Thelma could cook for them.

The ring of the doorbell signaled the end of the meeting, or at least a pause. Fen announced, "I'll get it. Ben Crump is supposed to stop by."

Ren turned to Bailey. "Who is Ben Crump?"

"A game warden."

"Is he cute?"

"He's Fen's age."

Ren let out a disappointed, "Oh."

Fen left the room and rounded a corner. He passed through the entry hall to the century-old front door, and swung it open. Before him stood a young man wearing jeans, boots, a baseball cap, and a collared shirt with the tail out. Green eyes stared at him. It only took a second before he matched a name to the face. "Officer West, you look different out of uniform. Come in."

"Thanks, Sheriff Maguire. I'm off duty, so it's John. I mean, that's my first name. I saw your truck parked out front and was wondering if you'd like to go to dinner."

Ren and Bailey picked that moment to come into the living room. The double pocket doors were open, which gave John a clear view of the two young women.

Fen didn't answer, but fixed his attention on John and how he reacted to seeing two attractive females his age. John looked first at Ren, then Bailey, and back at Ren. His gaze didn't shift as Ren closed the distance with hand extended. "Did I hear you say your name is John? That's such a solid name. It reminds me of an oak tree on my grandpa's ranch. I painted that tree." She held up her other hand. "Wait. I didn't paint the tree. I painted a painting of the tree." She tilted her head. "That doesn't sound right, either. Oh well, what do you do?"

"Uh...uh..."

"He's a cop," said Bailey. "Can't you tell by the haircut and the pistol under his shirt?"

This brought John out of his stupor. "Few girls would spot that. How'd you guess?"

"When you grow up on the streets of Houston, you learn to spot cops."

Fen jumped into the conversation. "I met John back in June. He was the first officer at the river."

"Yeah," said Bailey. "You taped off the area before they banished you to direct traffic. Fen said you did a good job and didn't complain. I'd have raised a stink."

"I was scared I'd make a mistake. Sheriff Maguire reminded me of what I needed to do."

"I doubt that," said Ren. "You look like a Leo to me. That means you're bold as a lion. When's your birthday?"

"I turned twenty-one in August."

"I knew it. You're John the Lionhearted." Instead of shaking hands, Ren curtsied. "And of what service may I be to you, Lord John?"

"Uh?"

Fen answered for him. "John came by to ask me to go to dinner with him. I'm expecting company, so why don't you three go?"

Ren clapped her hands. "That's a great idea." She looked at him with eyebrows raised in expectation. "Where are we going?"

"We could go to Pocket's Grill, which is only three blocks away, or we could drive into Bastrop."

Fen offered his opinion. "You'll like Pockets. They have good food and a bunch of movie memorabilia."

Ren grabbed Bailey's arm. "I'm starving. Let's go stuff our faces."

Bailey looked at John. "Do we need to meet you there?"

"My truck is old enough to have a bench seat. Plenty of room for three. I'll show you the sights of Smithville after we eat if you want to ride around."

"We do!" shouted Ren, as she pulled harder on Bailey's arm.

Fen explained as the duo of artists ran toward the kitchen. "They're staying in the rooms overlooking the backyard. You'd better run along and pick them up on 2nd Street."

John tilted his head. "Is Ren always so... bubbly?"

"You should see her after she eats chocolate-covered coffee beans."

John's smile widened. "That would be worth seeing. This town could use someone who isn't a stick in the mud." He extended his right hand to shake. "It's good to see you, Sheriff. Thanks again for helping me through my first major crime scene. The chief told me I did a good job."

Fen answered with a nod and a smile. "If you don't hurry, Ren may run to the restaurant just to beat you in the door."

"I've yet to be involved in a foot pursuit. That might be fun."

Fen allowed the double meaning to pass without comment. The front door closed and silence once again took the place of youthful exuberance. Lou's voice pierced the quiet. "He's a handsome young man, and Ren's wearing her heart on her sleeve. That's a dangerous combination."

"Bailey may be only a month and a half shy of twenty, but she's wise beyond her years. She'll minimize the damage to Ren if something goes wrong."

"I'm not so sure," said Lou. "John's name is on the list of suspects. The background information I collected on him has holes in it I intend to fill."

Thelma appeared from behind a corner. "I agree with Lou. A young man that good-looking can't be trusted. You heard him say his truck has a bench seat in the front. That's one of those SOB seats... scoot over, baby."

Fen raised a single eyebrow. "Is that the voice of experience I hear talking?"

"Don't you worry about my experience, or lack of it. Keep an eye on that young lady and that feller with a badge and gun. There are good cops and bad ones. I haven't been around him long enough to tell what kind he is."

A second ring of the doorbell brought the discussion to a close. "That should be Ben Crump," said Fen. "Do you two want me to talk to him in the living room or the dining room? I want to make sure you're comfortable when you listen."

Lou answered. "I'd like to sit at this table and drink a cup of coffee. Bring him in here so I can see him."

Thelma added, "I'll hear just fine from the kitchen. I like the way they built this house. There's plenty of walls to hide behind; no need for me to make up excuses to bring you things so I can snatch a sentence or two."

Fen groaned and went to the door.

Chapter Ten

Ben Crump wiped his boots on the welcome mat before entering. Fen greeted him and asked if he preferred coffee or something cold to drink. He chose water and said, "I've been checking fishing licenses all afternoon. Ninety-four degrees in the shade, and there's no shade on Lake Bastrop. It's supposed to cool off tonight, but that didn't help me today."

They reached the dining room and Ben came to a stop. "I didn't realize there were other guests staying here."

Fen flicked away his concern. "Ben, this is Lou Cooper. She's part of my team."

Lou extended a hand. "Nice to meet you, Ben. You've compiled an exemplary record as a game warden. I understand you've put in your paperwork for retirement."

Ben gave Lou a hard look before shifting his gaze to Fen. "I did that two days ago. How does she know?"

Fen chuckled. "Lou was a top investigative reporter in Dallas before some people in power suggested she take her skills elsewhere. She now covers what little news there is in Newman County until I need her to help me work on a case. I don't ask too many questions about her sources or methods of gathering information."

Ben hooked his thumbs in his gun belt. "I'm not sure I care for information in my personnel file becoming public knowledge."

Lou smiled. "It won't be." She paused. "At least, it won't be for a long time. Fen and I have an agreement concerning honest cops."

"Oh?" Suspicion laced his words. "I'd like to hear about that deal."

Fen placed a hand on Ben's shoulder. "Have a seat. I'll get you a glass of ice water." He shifted his gaze. "Lou, tell him what you do."

"I already have. I dig up background information for you. Sometimes, I write articles for newspapers if they help move the case forward. I also file away the details of the cases Fen solves. Someday I'll compile them into a book, or a series of books. That's my retirement plan."

"Do you use real names?"

"I won't use yours."

"Why not?"

Lou gave him a wide smile. "To begin with, Fen wouldn't want me to. That probably wouldn't stop me, but I still wouldn't. You're not interesting enough, so there's no advantage in using your real name. If you were a dirty cop, I would."

This brought a smile that parted Ben's lips. "You have a way with words."

Fen added, "There's someone else listening to us you need to know about." He directed his attention to the kitchen door and spoke a little louder. "Can you hear all right, Thelma?"

"Just fine."

Fen delivered the glass of water. "That's Sam's wife. She's my cook and housekeeper, not a normal part of my team, but I trust her and Sam more than anyone I know. Lou is the best there is for doing what you might call formal research. Thelma gathers information in a more personal way. Some might call it gossip."

Thelma looked into the dining room from the kitchen, over the swinging doors. "He's trying to say I can tell him what's going to be filed at the courthouse before it happens."

Ben gave a nod that said he understood but still frowned. "If I was already retired, I wouldn't mind speaking freely. Until then, perhaps Fen and I should go on the front porch to talk."

"Good idea," said Fen. "I'll take a mason jar full of cold water with me, too."

An evening breeze brought relief from the day's heat as Fen and Ben settled in rocking chairs. Ben closed his eyes as the wind rustled the leaves in mature pecan trees. "I'm looking forward to doing this daily."

"It gets old after a month or two."

"I'll take my chances."

The chairs went forward and back, making a pleasant creaking sound. Silence ruled until Fen broke it. "It seems the investigation stalled out after the district attorney determined Riley Eastham had a decent alibi."

"The chief of police is afraid he'll make another mistake. It would be a shame if he arrests another innocent person."

"Political pressure?"

Ben kept his eyes closed. "You should know all about that."

"I do, and I don't miss it one bit. Where's the most pressure coming from?"

"Directly, it's coming from several members of the city council."

"Who's the person pulling the strings?"

"Mildred Fox. All was going her way when they arrested Riley Eastham."

Fen waited a few seconds for Ben to elaborate. When he didn't, Fen said, "Tell me about Mildred."

"Do you want the long version?"

"The short one will do for now."

Ben opened his eyes and kept rocking. "Mildred Fox, eighty-five-year-old widow of Hank Fox. Hank had connections in the state highway department in Austin. He knew ahead of time about Highway 71 bypassing the town, so he bought up most of the land on both sides of the easement."

Fen considered the mostly undeveloped land. "There's not much out there yet."

Ben nodded. "That's because Mildred likes things the way they are."

"Ah. Who's next in line to inherit the land?"

"Only one son, named Clayton Fox. He's the town's dentist. Mildred is the self-appointed matriarch of Smithville and nemesis to anyone with the last name Eastham. It involves the decades-old squabble over the land grab by Mildred's late husband. Have Lou look for newspaper stories concerning the Highway 71 bypass."

Fen moved on. "I understand they identified the victim as Lee Grimes. He had quite the criminal record."

Ben stopped rocking. "No record of violence, but they should have put a revolving door on his jail cell. He was one of those guys who invented ways to break the law. If he'd worked a real job as hard as he did trying to beat the system, he'd have been rich. Hot checks, back when people wrote them, stealing anything that wasn't tied down. Scams, shams, and flim-flams. You name it and Lee would try it."

"He must have had plenty of enemies."

"Not as many as you'd think. He tried to steal in more ways than you can imagine, but he had a bad habit of getting caught."

Fen stilled his rocking. "He got in over his head with someone. The autopsy report said three stab wounds to the heart. One would have done it."

"I hadn't heard that," said Ben. "City police took over the case after I told them I'd received an anonymous tip about the original crime scene. That new officer, John West, found the knife."

Fen nodded. "He seems like a bright kid. I'm surprised he's working in such a small town."

"His mother lives here, too."

"Who's his mother?"

Ben chuckled. "Lou needs to do a better job on background checks. John's mother is Audrey West, the city attorney."

Fen realized too late that his mouth had hinged open. Ben glanced his way and chuckled. "You'd better shut that thing before a fly makes his home in there." Ben's laugh increased in volume.

Fen tried to redeem himself, and Lou, by offering an explanation. "Lou's not had much time to do background checks yet. I didn't think we'd be working this case after they arrested Riley Eastham. I'm sending Lou to Dallas to do more research on his alibi. Do you know how airtight it is?"

Ben shook his head. "I'm a lowly game warden who keeps his head down." He took a drink of water. "I can tell you this much. Riley has a reputation for being a tough businessman. If he was selling used cars, I'd buy a horse."

"Any history of violence?"

"Not from Riley. He's too cunning to get his hands dirty." Ben looked at the faded mural on the building across the street. "That doesn't apply to his only boy, Sonny. He's mean as a stepped-on water moccasin when he's drinking, which is way too often."

Fen joined Ben, looking at the building across the street. "That's about as mean as they come. Many arrests?"

"Plenty, but none since they released him from prison. He served two years on a three-year sentence for assault. It should have been aggravated assault with a deadly weapon, but Riley paid big money to a high-powered lawyer." He shot his gaze back to Fen. "Before you ask, Sonny stuck a knife in the belly of a high school senior who owed him money for drugs."

Fen's mind raced. The knife used to kill Lee Grimes belonged to Riley Eastham, but he claimed to be in Dallas at the time of the murder. There was evidence to support this, but for someone like Riley, enough money could buy testimonies to the contrary. Or, perhaps, his son used his father's knife to kill another known criminal who lived a mere fifteen miles west of Smithville.

Ben stood to leave. "Good luck catching the killer. Some people would say Lee Grimes wasn't much of a loss to society, but I kind of liked him. No person deserves to die the way he did."

"I agree, and thanks for the information. It gives us a place to start."

The two shook hands and Fen watched his friend climb into his game warden's pickup and drive away.

The squeak of the rocking chair didn't sound as pleasant when Fen returned to it. He needed to gather information about Sonny Eastham. But what was the best way to do it? Bailey was the obvious choice of the person most likely to get him to answer questions. She had the street smarts and could talk the language of someone who'd felt handcuffs on their wrists. Was it worth involving her? Probably not, but he also knew she'd find out about Sonny on her own. If Ben looked upon him as a suspect, half the town did, too.

For now, Fen would meditate on the information he'd gathered from Ben. Tomorrow morning was soon enough to discuss Riley Eastham and his boy, Sonny. The sun was below the horizon when Fen went back inside. Lou sat in the living room with her laptop. Fen waited until she raised her gaze to meet his and asked him, "Did you find out anything interesting from Ben?"

"Plenty. Focus on Riley Eastham and his boy, Sonny. The younger went to prison for stabbing someone."

"Interesting. That sounds like an interview for Bailey, unless you want me to talk to him."

"I'll let you know in the morning." He paused. "Aren't you going to the beer garden?"

"It takes three or four beers before men loosen up enough to talk. I'm waiting for it to get dark." She paused. "What about you?"

"I'm heading out now. There's a woman I want to talk to. Her son also interests me. He's currently giving Ren and Bailey a tour of Smithville."

"Ah. Ben told you about Audrey and John West. I'm working on their files now. Go get more information out of her. Computer searches aren't like searching records in a court-house. That's where the real gold is."

"I'll try, if she's there."

"She'll be there," said Lou with absolute confidence.

"What makes you say that?"

"She knows you're in town. Nothing much goes on in a town this size without the city attorney knowing about it."

Fen didn't argue the point, but he didn't particularly like Lou being right. Audrey had laid a trap for him back in June with the note recommending the restaurant. This time she probably knew he was in town already, and that he'd want to talk to her about her son and the case. He considered going somewhere else to eat, but that would be silly. Audrey was the logical source of information he needed.

Fen checked his hair in the foyer's antique mirror, then told

Thelma and Lou they could reach him on his cell phone before heading out the door and walking two blocks east.

The walk gave him a chance to allow his mind to roam where it wanted. There was too much about Audrey that he still didn't know, and that bothered him. What was there about the tiny town of Smithville that attracted her and her son? Was she hiding from something or someone? Was she somehow involved in the feud between the Foxes and the Easthams? If so, was she or her son somehow involved in the killing?

Fen brought his musings under control and opened the door to The Front Room Wine Bar. Once again, patrons filled all the seats at the bar. A quick scan of the room showed that Audrey wasn't among them.

As was his custom, Fen took a seat with his back to a wall, people-watched, and ordered a glass of iced tea. His gaze shifted when the front door opened. In walked Audrey, who took a direct path to where he sat. "You're back. Mind if I join you?"

Chapter Eleven

Fen stood and motioned to Audrey that she was welcome to occupy the chair on the opposite side of the table from him. She moved the chair to where the bar wouldn't be behind her. The closer proximity allowed a more private conversation but also put her within touching distance.

She'd already caught the attention of the server and he arrived soon after she settled. She looked up at the server. "Pull me a draft beer in a frozen mug."

The server stated the obvious. "Audrey, you look like you've been working cattle. Did Doc Fox con you into helping him again?"

"He did, and we're talking instead of you bringing me something to cut the dust."

"I'll be right back."

Fen had already noted how different Audrey looked from the last time they met. The cowboy-cut jeans were old and faded, as was the chambray long-sleeve shirt. Her scuffed boots bore dirt, age, and manure. She wore a baseball cap with her black hair in a ponytail sticking out the back. If she'd started the day wearing makeup, she wasted her time and money. Salt stains on her shirt and a dark line on her neck told their own story of how hard she'd worked.

Fen's thoughts drifted back in time to his wife, Sally. Her father, the biggest landowner in Newman County, made sure she knew how to ride a horse long before she could ride a bicycle. They received a wedding gift of four thousand acres of prime bottomland and woods.

The next thing Fen realized was Audrey snapping her fingers in front of his face. He directed his gaze to her as she said, "Earth to Fen. I don't know where you went, but it sure wasn't in this bar."

He croaked out, "Sorry. Sometimes my mind wanders."

She flashed a smile. "I thought you couldn't believe how ugly I am without makeup and after wallowing in a feedlot."

The next words jumped out before he could catch them. "I admire a woman who isn't pretentious."

Her gaze seemed to search his thoughts. Or was it his heart? She leaned back. "I'm not sure if you're being nice or if you need your vision checked."

It was time to move to firmer emotional ground. "How familiar are you with Riley Eastham?"

She gave him a sideways glance. "That was an abrupt transition. I thought we'd have at least ten or fifteen minutes of small talk before talking about the case." Her green eyes seemed to dance. "This should be when we discover how much we know about each other. Also, if we're going to lie."

Fen spurted out a laugh. "You'll have to forgive me. It's been a while since my last case. I'm out of practice. Do you want to start?"

"Let's take turns. I'll go first."

He nodded in agreement.

Audrey squared her shoulders. "James Fenimore Maguire.

Both parents are deceased. You graduated college after studying criminal justice and art. After ten years as a state trooper, you got in the way of a bullet meant for someone else. It did enough damage to your right knee that they gave you a medical retirement."

"I should have had a knee replacement. I limped needlessly for another ten years."

"But you weren't idle. After limping around, the people of Newman County elected you sheriff, then reelected you. Ten more years passed, and you made a great reputation for yourself, both as sheriff and an artist."

"Not good enough."

"Extenuating circumstances," said Audrey. "Your wife died and her father blamed you."

Fen spoke through clenched teeth. "He said I didn't try hard enough to talk her into having a second heart transplant."

Audrey continued. "He had money enough to swing the election in favor of his daughter. That turned into a disaster for the county. She didn't last long as sheriff. It's still unclear to me why you didn't run for sheriff again."

"My painting became more important."

Audrey gave him a sideways glance. "That's only part of the reason, but we'll let that go for now."

The server arrived with Audrey's beer. "Sorry it took so long. Lucy is having a hard time keeping up tonight."

"Thanks. Do I need to order another now or wait a few minutes?"

He looked at the bar. "How thirsty are you?"

"Dry as a West Texas dust storm."

"I'll put in the order."

"Do you want to order supper?"

Audrey looked at Fen. "How hungry are you?"

"I snacked all the way to town. What about you?"

She shook her head. "I don't eat heavy on days when I get hot. How 'bout we share some super nachos?"

"That works for me."

The server left, and Audrey took three swallows from her icy mug. She lowered it to the coaster on the table. "My goodness, that's what I needed." She folded her hands in front of her. "Your turn, Sheriff. Let's see what you know about me."

Fen lifted a single eyebrow. "I'm afraid it's not much. At least not yet."

Audrey raised her eyebrows in surprise but said nothing.

Fen hurried to speak. "Audrey Jean West." He paused. "It's not polite to discuss a woman's age, but you're roughly the same age I am. Adopted at birth by Lee and Elizabeth West. No information yet on birth parents. You had an otherwise normal childhood, except you're a chronic overachiever. Valedictorian of your high school class. You then graduated in the top ten percent at UT in Austin. You stayed at UT and went to law school."

Fen took a breath. "This is where things get murky. The information I have on you is incomplete."

"Why is that?"

"A simple matter of not enough time. In fact, I didn't know John West is your son until today. Did you know he stopped by to see me this afternoon?"

Her ponytail swung as she gave a slight shake of her head. "I've been looking at cattle rumps all day."

Fen chuckled. "I guess sons don't tell their mothers everything they're doing."

"You should know. Bailey's not your daughter, but she might as well be. Does she tell you everything she's doing?"

"Not always. But I know where she is now."

"Where?"

"With John."

"You're joking."

Fen held up three fingers. "Boy Scout's honor. Bailey and her friend Ren are with him at either Pockets Grille or riding around town." He paused, then said, "He seemed more interested in Ren than Bailey."

Audrey stiffened. "What can you tell me about this Ren girl?"

"She's a very cute, gregarious young lady. Like Bailey, she's an artist but paints in a completely different medium. Murals on buildings are her specialty."

Fen noticed Audrey's scowl. "You don't look pleased."

Audrey grabbed her mug and took a long drink before answering. "I'm probably projecting my past hurts onto my son. He's not like I was when I was in law school."

"Oh?"

Audrey ran a finger around the rim of her mug. "The pressure to finish near the top of my class took its toll. Friday night parties were a relief valve for many of us. I made a choice that altered the trajectory of my life."

"Ah," said Fen.

She pushed what remained of the unfinished beer away from her. "John's birth father wouldn't do the honorable thing, which was fine with me. Incompatible doesn't come close to describing our personalities. His rich Houston family had political aspirations for their son. A county-lawyer wife with a mind of her own and a love child didn't meet their qualifications. All it took to solve their problem was generous child support and a college education for John. They paid it in cash. I graduated, passed the bar, and established my practice."

"Does John know who his birth father is?"

"No, and he never will. That was part of the deal I made with the lawyers. They provided a home in Houston for me to live in the last month of my pregnancy. I had a live-in midwife and a doctor on call. John came right on schedule and there were no complications."

"What about the birth certificate?"

"One exists, but the attorneys made sure it omitted the father. There's also an adoption certificate with my name as the mother and *Unknown* as the father. It's not that hard for money and skilled lawyers to fix people's problems."

"The family must have really wanted their son to have a spotless record."

"You'd know their last name if I said it." She paused. "By the way, if you breathe a word of what I told you, I'll deny it. There's nothing to prove who John's father is, and I guarantee he'll never submit to a DNA test."

Fen held up his palms. "No one will hear it from me. Now, have we talked long enough that I can get back to my original question about Riley Eastham?"

The server approached with Audrey's next beer. She looked at the mug and then at Fen. "Do you want it?"

Fen wagged his head. "I didn't work cattle today. It's all yours."

Audrey looked up at the server. "Give it to someone at the bar with compliments from a secret admirer. It will start a juicy rumor."

Fen sputtered out a laugh. "There's a touch of mischief in you, counselor."

"And you're a good listener, Sheriff Maguire."

He gave her a mock hurt look. "Please, Audrey. Call me Fen."

She placed her hand on his. "You know more about me than my son does. If I call you Fen, there's no telling what other secrets you'll find out about me."

Fen eased his hand away and picked up his tea glass. "I'll settle for information about Riley Eastham."

Her tone changed to that of an attorney giving a guarded answer. "Riley is a client of mine, so I can't go into details about his business dealings."

"Are you his only attorney?"

"No. He has business holdings in Dallas, Austin, and Bastrop. I only help him with local real estate matters. He prefers to use local attorneys in whatever city his business is located. That doesn't count the defense attorney who sued the chief of police and the city."

Fen knew everything Audrey said was public record and safe. He needed to dig deeper. "What are his chances of winning the case against the city?"

Once again, she proved to be evasive. "I can't really comment on pending litigation."

"Of course not. Sorry I asked." He took a drink of iced tea and tried to extract something from her by changing tactics. "Let's say I wanted to interview Riley. Do you think he'd talk to me?"

"It all depends. Some people say he's an easy man to dislike. Others go further and describe him as hot-headed and demanding. Many regard him as an upstanding businessman who's trying to drag this city out of the twentieth century." She leaned toward him. "If you talk to him, make it short and to the point."

After he gave her a single nod, Audrey leaned back. Fen then said, "I understand John found the knife in the city-owned field by the river."

"That's because the city doesn't keep it mowed and none of the other officers wanted to go home covered with chigger bites."

"The information I received said Riley wouldn't answer questions about his knife. Did he lose it and someone else found it?"

"Beats me. That would be a good question to ask him, but I doubt he'll tell you anything."

"What's your opinion of Bonnie Sterling, Riley Eastham's girlfriend?"

Audrey shrugged. "I barely know her, and they're engaged." She turned her head toward the kitchen door. "How long does it take to fix a platter of nachos?"

"You should know. This is your town."

"Not exactly *mine*. It's a temporary stop on my journey."

The kitchen door opened and out came the server carrying their order. Audrey flashed him a smile. "These are worth the wait. You're in for a treat."

Fen decided not to press her for more information. He had all week, and it was only Sunday night.

Chapter Twelve

F en put his bare feet on the rug by the bed in the pre-dawn darkness but didn't rise. Something wasn't right. Not physically, but some unseen force had caused his mind to jump from subject to subject and steal what should have been a full night's sleep. He had hoped to experience a rerun of the dreamless slumber he'd experienced back in June.

He whispered in the dark. "No chance of that after Thelma met me at the front door and grilled me like I was a bank robber. She was so intense that I forgot to ask about her trip to the grocery store."

He made a mental spreadsheet and logged everything that had pushed sleep away from his bed. "Today's painting class." He shook his head. Who was he trying to kid? He might have spent ten minutes of his night going over what he'd say and do. He hadn't even memorized the names of the students.

His thoughts shifted to Bailey and Ren. He'd seen John's truck parked on the street near their rooms, but he hadn't checked on them. "I should have done that." He thought about his words and corrected himself. "No, they're all adults." He puffed out his cheeks. "I don't see how parents know when or how to release their children." He wondered if all parents or guardians were sleep-deprived.

Audrey's name went into the next box on his spreadsheet. He had to admit that processing the barrage of information about her had occupied most of the time he spent staring at the ceiling. How had he not seen the resemblance between her and her son? Perhaps it was because she'd awakened something in him that he thought died with Sally. "Admit it," he said to himself. "It's hard not to get lost in those eyes. The rest of her is worth a second look, too." A wave of guilt washed over him. "Sorry, Sally. You know I prefer blue eyes and blond hair." He placed his late wife's name in the next box and felt even more guilt because she didn't take up more of last night's thoughts. He wondered if people might be right about him moving on someday. "Nah. I'm a one-woman man. End of conversation."

The sound of creaking wood caused him to lift his head. "That's Thelma," he said in a quiet whisper. The creaking stairs confirmed she was awake and heading down to start her day. It didn't surprise him she'd be the first up and dressed. Not only did she take exorbitant pride in her work, she had an insatiable thirst for keeping tabs on anyone in what she considered her territory. He'd spent a considerable amount of time last night wondering if he'd made a mistake by including her this week.

Thelma felt she could test boundaries when not at home. Was the juice going to be worth the squeeze this time, or would he have to send her home again? Time would tell.

Fen slipped into jeans and padded his way barefoot down the noisy stairs. He made it to the single-serve coffee maker before Thelma came from the kitchen. "The real coffee will be ready shortly. I don't trust that stuff they put in plastic. Those contraptions sound like an old man clearing his throat and spitting when that dinky thing finishes."

She took a breath. "The owners of this place aren't all bad. They make coffee in an old-school Sunbeam percolator. You go back to your room and start your time with Sally. I'll bring real coffee to you in your favorite mug from home."

He considered putting a pod in the machine and brewing his first cup of the day just for spite. On second thought, that was silly for a number of reasons. First, she'd gone to the extra effort of rising earlier than usual to serve him. Second, she'd brought his favorite mug. Somehow, coffee tasted better in it. Finally, he needed to save his words of correction for when she really stepped over the line.

Instead, he asked, "Are there any lights on yet in Bailey's or Ren's rooms?"

"No, and it ain't no wonder. I had to run that boy out of Bailey's room at eleven o'clock. Those girls were jabbering like magpies and they need to paint today. Besides, it's not proper for a man to be in a young lady's bedroom."

"That bedroom has a small kitchenette. It's more like an efficiency apartment."

Thelma wagged her head as she scowled. "If there's a bed when you walk in the door, it's a bedroom, and all three were on it."

Fen groaned, knowing he'd hear more about this from Bailey. He turned and left. First light hadn't pierced the dark and already he faced a day of needless fatigue, a pushy housekeeper, and two offended artists. He wasn't off to a good start.

Things improved marginally when he received his mug filled with coffee that somehow tasted better than what Thelma made back home. Was it the water or perhaps the vintage percolator that made the difference? He'd consider that later.

For now, he placed Sally's framed photo on a table between the wing-back chairs and told her all about last night's meeting with Audrey. He described his walk in the dark back to The Katy House. "It occurred to me I didn't ask what brought her and her son to Smithville. This isn't the county seat, so she has to drive to Bastrop to file papers at the court-house or go to court. From the little information in her file, this isn't where her adoptive parents live." He took a sip of coffee. "And why would her son want to start his career in such a small town?"

He took a longer drink from his mug. "I didn't like her story about falsifying John's birth certificate. If she did that for money, what else might she do?" A look into the mug showed a few grounds stuck to the side. "Something's not right about Audrey, and I need to find out what it is."

Time had a habit of accelerating when he had a lot on his mind and needed to talk to Sally. By the time he showered, shaved, and dressed, it was six-fifteen. He took his mug and walked down the squeaky stairs that ensured Thelma was waiting for him. He spoke before the heel of his boot touched the last step. "Are the girls in the dining room?"

"They left for the coffee shop like you told them to. Didn't so much as darken the back doorstep before they sneaked out like a couple of burglars." She huffed. "I'm telling you, Fen. That boy and his green-eyed mother aren't to be trusted."

Fen needed to go, but not before he extracted something useful from Thelma. "How was your trip to the grocery store yesterday afternoon?"

"Not as good as I'd hoped. I invited a lady over for coffee this morning. I think she knows most of what's going on in town. She retired from working at City Hall two years ago and attends the Naomi and Ruth Bible study group at church. Those are pretty good credentials."

"Find out about long-standing hard feelings between two families in town."

Thelma held up both palms to blunt any further words. "I told you before that I'll do things my way and you use your fancy detective skills. We'll see who gets the most information."

"Gathering information is all I want you to do." He gave her a stare intended to communicate how serious he was. "What I don't want you to do is jump to conclusions about someone's guilt or innocence. That includes the city attorney and Officer West."

It was always hard to tell with Thelma if his warnings penetrated her tough outer shell. He didn't need another thing on his mental spreadsheet so he turned toward the door. "I'll be back for breakfast and a sack lunch around eight."

She spoke to him as his hand touched the doorknob. "I'm cooking you and the girls a full breakfast, so don't eat any pastries."

"I'm going to talk to Bailey and Ren." He stopped and turned to look at her. "I may not go to the bakery this morning, but I'll eat what I want when I decide to."

Thelma's harumph and the sound of the kitchen doors swinging reverberated in his mind. He'd be walking a fine line this week of keeping control of this investigation, as well as his own freedom.

Streaks of light shot through low clouds to the east as he walked and put his mind on the next conversation of the day. He hoped the first words out of Bailey weren't a full-throated complaint about Thelma invading the privacy of her room.

The look on her face when he entered the coffee shop snuffed out his hopes. Instead of going directly to her and Ren, he approached the counter and ordered a small cup of coffee. It came in a white paper cup with a corrugated cardboard sleeve to help prevent burns. He took one sip and winced. The coffee didn't compare to what he'd enjoyed earlier.

Bailey sat on the last cushion of a couch that looked like a college apartment reject. Ren occupied a chair of similar quality that almost touched the couch near Bailey. Fen sank onto the couch, but not too close to Bailey. He waited, but not for long. The eruption came through clenched teeth. "Send her home or we're leaving."

Fen used the prop of the hot coffee to delay his response. He took another sip, then winced again as steam rose from the super-heated cup of stimulant. Ren's warning came too late. "I burned the fuzz off my tongue, too."

"Thelma told me she asked John to leave last night."

Bailey's dagger stare fixed on Fen. "She barged in without knocking and all but accused us of having some sort of wild party. That was before she checked the refrigerator to see if we had beer."

Ren lowered her chin. "She calmed down after John left."

Bailey hadn't finished. "She's so 1950s in the way she thinks. Doesn't she know people our age sit on beds to watch television? That's all we were doing and the only items of clothing we took off were our shoes." Her volume rose. "There we were, all three of us lined up on the bed." She used her hands to show their placement. "I was on one side, John was on the other, and Ren was the peanut butter in the middle of the sandwich. In comes the Gestapo."

Fen raised his hand and lowered it slowly in a calm-down gesture, then spoke in a soft voice. "Here's what I want both of you to do."

"Didn't you hear me?" said Bailey in a loud whisper. "Either Thelma goes home or the only things you'll see of us are our taillights."

Fen snapped back with force. "Knock it off." He allowed

the sharp words to sink in. "Thelma had no right to do what she did. I'll talk to her and tell her to stay out of your rooms, but you aren't running away. There's a job, and you both agreed to help me do it." He calmed his voice. "I need both of you, and Lou, and Thelma to help me."

"But—"

"No buts. We're all staying and solving this case. You two eat something here. Make friends. At nine o'clock, you'll be on time at the Lost Pines Artisans Gallery on Main Street. There's not much room in the building, so I'll make it short and everyone but Ren will go to one of four locations to sketch."

Ren held up her hand. "John introduced me to the lady who owns the building with the mural. I have her permission to repaint the mural as long as I don't make any changes without talking to her first."

Fen nodded his approval. Something had finally gone right. He then looked at Bailey, who still had her arms crossed over her chest. "I hope you both realize that Thelma was trying to protect you. She's the way she is because she didn't have anyone who cared about her until Sally took her under her wing. She saw something good in Thelma. It took me a while, but I see it too."

Bailey uncrossed her arms. "I'll stay unless she busts into my room again."

Fen knew a storm still raged inside Bailey, but the tornado had gone back into the clouds.

"By the way," said Fen. "Did you learn anything from John last night?"

Bailey rolled her eyes. "Not much."

She tilted her head toward Ren, who looked away sheepishly. "I can't help it that I talk more than I should. That goes double when I'm nervous or excited. The sentences come out of my mouth like water going over Niagara Falls."

Bailey leaned back on the couch. "John and I did a lot of listening. Ren finally ran out of words about five minutes before Thelma busted in."

Fen closed his eyes, took in a deep breath, and wondered if he'd have to fight headwinds all week.

Chapter Thirteen

Leaving Bailey and Ren in the coffee shop, Fen marched to the bakery and ate a cinnamon roll. It was an insignificant gesture of independence, but it felt good all the same. He only drank a few sips of the sub-par coffee while sitting on the dilapidated couch with Bailey, so the one he ordered with his pastry counted as his second cup of the day.

Conversation was sparse in the bakery until he recognized a woman who breezed in with her gaze fixed on the counter. She placed an order then turned to face the small dining area. Her eyebrows shot up.

The woman behind the counter spoke in a loud voice. "Here's your order, Bonnie. Are you sure you don't want something else?"

"No thanks. Riley's back from Dallas and threw a fit when I didn't have one of your éclairs for his breakfast."

Fen stood as Bonnie Sterling approached and addressed him. "I don't know if you remember me or not, Sheriff Maguire."

"I remember you, Bonnie. You and Riley were at the river back in June."

She offered a weak smile. "You have an excellent memory. Riley tells me I have a face that's easy to forget." She forced a laugh. "I guess he can say that since we're engaged now."

Fen hoped his surprise didn't show. From the way Riley had spoken to her that day in June, he wouldn't have guessed the couple was engaged. He smiled and said, "Congratulations on the upcoming wedding. Have you set a date?"

"Not yet."

A loud truck passed by and Bonnie raised her gaze to the window. It was then he noticed she wasn't wearing an engagement ring. Perhaps she didn't wear her ring all the time in an effort to protect it. Or, perhaps Riley and Bonnie didn't define the word engaged the same way.

She brought her attention back to him. "I need to go, but I'll see you at nine. I'm so excited about learning more about landscapes from such a talented artist."

Internally, Fen wanted to kick himself. It hadn't occurred to him that one or more of the class participants could be a source of information for the murder case. Why hadn't he memorized the names of the people who'd signed up for the class? It was this lack of attention to detail that could cause a guilty person to go free. He'd need to up his game.

A parting smile preceded his words. "I look forward to our week working together to create something memorable. Be sure to bring your sketch pad and a cell phone. You'll need to take pictures."

The trip to the bakery improved Fen's outlook on the day. He now had what could prove to be an inside track to information on Riley Eastham. On the way back to The Katy House, another thought crossed his mind. Even if Riley was in Dallas at the time of the murder, what about Bonnie? Did she go with him, or did she remain in Smithville? It was a long shot, but any woman willing to fetch her boyfriend a single éclair to round out his breakfast might perform a more unsavory task for him.

***

THE UNMISTAKABLE SMELL of fried bacon hit Fen as soon as he stepped into the bed-and-breakfast. Last night's shared deluxe nachos were long gone. The gooey cinnamon roll tempered his appetite, but not enough to where he couldn't enjoy eggs, bacon, and a single biscuit. He walked into the dining room as Thelma called out from the kitchen. "You're cutting it close this morning. Where are the girls?"

"They're not coming."

She didn't explode, but sometimes Thelma's silence spoke louder than her rants. It usually meant a timed-delay blast. Fen had prepared for it and walked into the kitchen to strike a preemptive blow. He set his jaw and spoke. "I told them to eat somewhere else this morning."

Her wall of silence remained, so he kept talking. "We may think of Bailey and Ren as girls, but they're full-grown women. Both are earning their own way through life and they expect to be treated as adults."

Thelma found words to counter his. "Baily's nineteen and Ren's only a year older. I'll consider them women when they're twenty-one."

Fen shook his head. "They each earn enough to live wherever they want and they're adults in the eyes of the law. They're both women, no matter what you think or say."

The words and tone stopped Thelma for a few seconds. "If they were responsible, mature women, they'd not have been in bed with that boy last night."

"On the bed, not in it. There's a big difference, and that boy is a man. You coming through their door uninvited is why they're not coming for breakfast. If you do it again, you'll run both of them off and I'll lose two people who came to help me. They're serious and so am I. Stay out of their rooms this week."

She took a step back from the stove. "What about me cleaning and making beds? I thought that was one of my jobs."

"Things are different when we're away from home working on a case. You can clean my room as much as you want, but you'll need to ask Lou, Bailey, and Ren how often they want you in their rooms."

"What about fresh towels?"

"Ask them. Don't be surprised if they use the same towel all week. Also, expect all of us to miss meals. That includes you. If you need to miss cooking us a meal to gather information, do it."

Thelma's hard shell showed a fracture when her chin quivered. "But I promised Miss Sally that I'd take care of you."

"And sometimes taking care of people means giving them space. That's what I'm trying to tell you. Give us space to work this week."

He took the harshness out of his voice. "Try to look at your time here as being on a working vacation. You have extra time to do all the snooping you want."

Lou chose that moment to walk into the kitchen carrying a cup of coffee. Thelma narrowed her gaze. "Where'd you get that?"

"From the dining room. That maker is simple enough that even I can make a cup of coffee I can't see through. I set the machine to eight ounces and used two pods in a big mug."

Fen gave Thelma a hard look. "This is your first chance to practice giving someone space."

Thelma closed her eyes. She opened them and asked, "Do you want breakfast this morning, Miss Lou?"

"I'll take whatever you're offering."

"You'll get more than Mr. Fen. He's already had a cinnamon roll at the bakery."

Fen chuckled. Not only had Thelma gotten in the last word, but she'd busted him for ignoring her command to abstain from pastries. What really amazed him was she hadn't mentioned it prior to Lou's arrival. She was a cagey old fox who knew she had a lecture coming.

With things back on an even keel, Fen and Lou went into the dining room as Thelma completed preparations and served breakfast. He pointed to an open chair. "Join us. It will save you from straining to hear what we're talking about."

"Don't mind if I do. After all, Miss Lou was up all night tapping on her computer. I'd like to hear what she found out."

Fen's fork hovered over the plate of bacon and two medium fried eggs. "I hope she discovered more about John West and his mother, Audrey."

Thelma's eyes widened.

Fen dove back into his meal.

Thelma made her presence known. "Don't you dangle a carrot like that in front of me, Mr. Fen. What's the story concerning John?"

Lou squinted. "I smell something juicy." She shifted her gaze to meet his. "I suspect you found out more about them last night than I did. Will I be able to use what you're about to tell us?"

"Not unless you want to be sued for everything you own, or ever will own. Besides, I promised her my lips were sealed." Fen gave only the basics of what Audrey had told him last night. Despite Lou and Thelmas's insistence on details, he skirted their questions with minimal answers, but still left one cold egg on his plate. No matter, the large cinnamon roll sat heavily on his stomach. He ended the explanation with, "John will never know who his biological father is. Neither will we. Some secrets are better off left alone."

Thelma scrunched her nose like she smelled a foul odor. "I don't like beds left unmade and things that don't add up."

Fen shrugged. "It's possible Audrey doesn't know who John's father is."

Lou had the answer. "Audrey had a brief marriage. When I say brief, I mean it lasted only long enough to get divorced."

Fen rubbed his chin. Audrey hadn't told him the full story. There existed another layer of duplicity. If attorneys went to such lengths to hide John's father's identity by fabricating adoption papers, why not put another layer of distance between them by giving Audrey fake wedding and divorce certificates?

Thelma wagged a finger at him. "That woman lawyer is too slick for my liking. You be careful."

Fen had more to say, mainly to Lou. "I ran into Bonnie Sterling at the bakery this morning. She's taking my art class. Did you do a background check on her?"

"I'm going to the courthouse in Bastrop this morning to verify what I know about her and Riley Eastham. When do you want me to go to Dallas?"

Fen had already mulled this question over in his mind and had an answer. "We'll discuss that tonight. We need to let Thelma find out what she can about the feud between the Eastham and Fox families. If it's still ongoing, plan on a trip to Dallas tomorrow."

Lou had one more thing to add. "When you're talking to Bonnie today, don't forget to ask her about Riley's son. He's a rotten apple with a worm in it."

Fen shifted his gaze between the two women. "Anything else before I leave?"

Thelma held a palm against her cheek. "I may be out-of-pocket today. I was eating a piece of peanut brittle last night and it pulled off a crown. There's supposed to be a dentist in this town, if I can get in to see him."

Fen sat up straight. "There is a dentist, and his name is Clayton Fox. He was on the trash clean-up crew that found the body in the river."

Lou added, "Dr. Fox is the son of Mildred Fox, who controls much of what goes on in this town."

Thelma held up a hand to blunt any words. "Don't say it. I'll come back tonight with more information about him than both of you."

Chapter Fourteen

P arked cars and pickup trucks made a long line down one side of Main Street at 9:00 a.m. Fen, and those enrolled in the class, shoehorned their way into the small showroom that displayed the works of local artists. He gained their attention by issuing a sharp whistle. "Thank you for coming. I planned on having a brief lecture, but now I realize we don't have room for that to be practical. No worries. Artists need to be flexible. That goes double and triple if you want to paint outdoors. It's difficult to master landscapes because the light and weather are constantly changing."

He took in an oversized breath and continued. "Our goals for today are as follows. First: You'll pick a location to paint. There are four to choose from. The first is a long, narrow lake that's south of town. There's an active railroad that runs by it. I'm sure I don't have to say this... but stay off the tracks."

Chuckles could be heard across the room.

A hand went up. "Can we include the train in the painting?"

"That's up to you, but remember that I designed this course

to help you develop your skills with landscapes. You can have anything man-made to help you tell a story, but make it a minor character. Focus on the sky, land, and nature."

Heads nodded, so he continued. "The second location is a river scene. There's a large opening that gives a long view of the Colorado. The advantage of this spot is you'll stand on a raised concrete platform. You won't have to worry about chiggers or ants nibbling on your ankles. Although, I can't make promises that mosquitoes or flies won't attack. I recommend you take insect repellent, no matter which location you choose.

"The next location is the lake at Buescher State Park. There's plenty of space to paint and the park has restrooms. You'll need to purchase a pass for each day you go there to paint."

Many heads nodded when he mentioned the proximity to restrooms.

"Finally," he announced. "If you stay on the blacktop road that runs by Buescher State Park, you'll see miles of open fields with the park as a distant backdrop."

A voice called out. "Which location would you choose?"

Fen considered the question before saying. "That's like asking a writer if they prefer short stories, novellas, novels, or epic novels. The river setting is a short story, the lake at Buescher State Park is a novella, Long Lake south of town is a novel, and the open fields southeast of the state park could fill thousands of pages. Each is an excellent choice, depending on what story you want your painting to tell."

Fen nodded to Bailey. She moved to the front of the gathering. "I have enlarged photos of the locations. Use them to decide where you want to paint. I'll set them up on easels outside the shop."

Before more hands went up, Fen added, "If you change your mind after going to a location, that's fine." He paused.

"However, I've found that my first choice is usually the best. Not always, but most of the time."

Bonnie Sterling raised her hand. "What do we do if we can't decide by looking at the photos?"

"You may have to visit all the locations."

"But how will I know?"

Fen both hated and loved this question, and he'd heard it many times before. "This may sound strange, but go with your gut. There will be something about a place that will either want you to paint it, or it won't. Don't force the issue or overthink it. The best paintings tell stories, reveal secrets, and make people feel something."

A hush fell over the room, so Fen continued. "After you settle on a location, you have two other assignments today. The first is to take a photo of what you're going to paint every hour. Study these photos tonight and tomorrow morning. Pay particular attention to how light plays off the landscape. Stay until dusk if you need to, or get up early and catch the sunrise if you think that will give you the best results."

He gulped a breath. "Finally, draw the scene you're going to paint on a sketch pad. If there are objects that stand out to you, draw them separately in greater detail. Determine your horizon line and where to crop the edges."

He turned his back to the artists and looked outside. "It's a great day to be outside. Detailed directions to the four locations are on the table by the door." He held one up. "I'll come by to check on everyone throughout the day."

Some artists took only a brief look at the enlarged photos before walking to their vehicles. Others studied the photos like they were ancient documents holding a secret that would yield untold riches. Many sought opinions, which Fen found humorous and a waste of time. If they'd paid attention, they would have understood the importance of a place speaking to them in a way that was too deep for words. He could almost guarantee the consensus seekers would produce mediocre, forgettable paintings.

Bailey stood to one side, observing the last group and smiling. She'd spent enough time under his tutelage to understand the simple fact that good works come from a place of deep feeling.

Fen motioned for her to follow him to a place out of earshot. He whispered, "I want you to follow Bonnie Sterling."

"Why?"

"Her fiancé is Riley Eastham."

Her eyebrows shot up. "He's the one who found the body."

Fen nodded to keep from having to use words.

"Wasn't her name on the list of people picking trash from the river?"

He turned to face away from the crowd. "She claims to be his fiancée, but I'm not sure he agrees. Send me a text and let me know what location she chooses. I'll spend a little extra time with her today. Be careful how you get to know her. She won't suspect you unless you ask too many questions."

"Which one is she?"

Fen turned around and spun back. "She's gone." A white SUV passed by. "That's her. If she turns right at the next block, she's going to either the lake south of town or the park where they found the body."

Bailey spoke over her shoulder. "Don't forget to gather the photos and easels. I'll text you when I find her."

Two artists, a husband and wife, were the last to finish looking at the photos of the four sites. Each had their own idea of the best location and didn't mind expressing their opinion. They debated an additional ten minutes, with arms flailing and voices raised. The only vehicles left in front of the gallery were a Tesla and Fen's truck when he loaded the easels and photos and made for the location south of town.

It came as a surprise that almost half the class chose the first location. Most seemed taken by the idea of incorporating the railroad track in their painting to help tell a story. They were flocking together instead of finding an original story or perspective. This didn't surprise him, as finding something unique in the ordinary was beyond many people.

He spent time with each artist, trying to catch their vision for what they wanted to express. Some knew. Most didn't. He almost overlooked a woman who'd separated herself from the others and walked several hundred yards down the bank of the lake. He followed a seldom-used path until he reached her. "Isn't your name Milly Eubanks?"

"I'm impressed that you took the time to learn our names."

Fen touched the brim of his straw cowboy hat to acknowledge her words. "What made you choose this spot?"

She pointed. "The path leads down to the water instead of going along the bank. It's probably an old trail that cattle used to get a drink." She pointed. "That was before someone put up that fence, but I can still see the place where the trail meets water. That spot represents birth." She pointed again. "There's a dead tree on the other bank." She spread her fingers and gave a slow wave over the expanse before them. "In between the banks is water, which represents the life we live. I see a trail that leads to birth, a life lived, and a person's inevitable death."

Fen swallowed. "If you capture that on canvas, you'll make a very good living." They spent a considerable amount of time discussing the finer points of composing and layering the work. He finished the conversation by saying. "Keep doing what you're doing. I'll try to get back to you and the others today, but time is slipping by."

She smiled. "I'd paint a rushing mountain stream to represent that."

He tipped his hat a second time and walked to his truck. On the way, he looked at his phone to check the time. It was already past noon. He hadn't intended to spend so much time at the first location, but at least he'd consulted almost half the participants, and lunch awaited him in his truck. He'd eat while driving to the park by the river. It was then he looked at his phone again and noticed he'd missed a text from Bailey.

help get here fast.

Thoughts of lunch took flight as his tires threw rocks and dirt, then squealed as he turned from the gravel road onto Highway 71. It seemed like half an eternity, but it took less than seven minutes for him to arrive at the river and come to a noisy stop in the parking lot that served the overlook of the river. He bounded out of his truck as Bailey took fast steps toward him.

"What's wrong?"

Bailey held up an index finger over her mouth to signal him to be quieter. She then signaled him to stay where he was.

Heavier than normal breathing and an accusation marked her arrival. "Why didn't you come sooner?"

"I was talking to students and didn't want to be rude, so I left my phone in the truck." His gaze shifted to the deck overlooking the river. "What happened and where's Bonnie?"

"That creepy son of Riley Eastham's came and told her to get home. Riley wanted her to fix their lunch. She took off like someone lit a string of firecrackers under her."

Fen noticed Bailey's hands shaking. "What did Sonny do to you?"

"He would have done more if a fisherman hadn't pulled up. I don't scare easy but Sonny is bad news."

"Details," said Fen in a no-nonsense voice.

Bailey gave a quick nod. "It started with looks. As soon as Bonnie left, he moved in. You know, his eyes roved over me and stared where they shouldn't. He looked at my left hand and asked what was wrong with it. I told him a burn caused it. He wanted details."

She paused, so Fen asked, "What did you tell him?"

"I told him some of the gas got on me when I poured gasoline on the last guy who looked at me the way he was and set him on fire."

"Did that slow him down?"

Her head wagged side to side. "Not a bit. His breath smelled like cigarettes and beer. He pinned me against the railing and put his hand..." The words trailed off as her eyes clouded.

Fen had to look away as guilt and anger fought for preeminence. He became aware she was talking again.

"The only thing that saved me was a man getting out of his boat. He had a pistol in a shoulder holster. Sonny saw him and backed away. He then looked at the parking lot and said he knew my truck and where I was staying. He told me to expect a late-night visitor."

Fen looked into blue eyes brimming with unshed tears. "I'll take care of him."

Bailey swiped at a tear coursing down her cheek and put steel in her voice. "I want a pistol. You already taught me how to shoot. I won't have nightmares the rest of my life because of what a low-life like Sonny Eastham might do to me."

"I said I'll take care of him."

"Like you didn't do today?"

The statement hit Fen like a sandbag dropped from the

second story of a building. He pulled a hand down his face. "Go back to the bed-and-breakfast and tell Thelma what happened. You'll be safe with her."

"Are you sure?"

"She never leaves home without her derringer."

Bailey's eyes widened. "I never knew she was packing."

"You don't know when I'm carrying either."

"Are you now?"

"Yes, but I don't always."

"Then what about me?"

Fen shook his head. "Spend the afternoon with Thelma."

"I'd rather follow you to the state park and paint there."

The idea wasn't without merit, especially if he could complete two phone calls and put a plan to protect Bailey in motion. "Give me a minute to think about it."

Fen took off his hat and wiped sweat from his forehead. He'd made it a habit to pick his battles with the women in his life. Losing a skirmish or two wasn't bad if he could win when it really mattered. He decided she would be safe at the park. "I'll relent this time. The only condition is you have to be close to at least two other artists."

"How close?"

"Sight and sound close."

A weak smile crept onto Bailey's countenance. "Will you tell me your plan?"

"You'll know by the time you drive home today. Follow me and we'll get you set up."

Chapter Fifteen

Fen's anger burned white hot as he drove to the next location, checking his rearview mirror to make sure Bailey was still behind him. She wasn't his daughter, but he was protective of her like a father. The thought of the ex-con threatening her wasn't something he'd put up with. A plan fell into place. It should work.

He and Bailey already had their passes that allowed them to visit any state park, so checking in at the gate was easy. Once through, he pulled into a parking lot and hopped out of his truck. Bailey's window came down with a whirring sound. "Why are we stopping here?"

"I thought you wanted to paint here."

"I changed my mind. No lake scenes, and I'm not about to paint the river. That place gives me the creeps. I'm going back on the road we turned off of. There's a great place to set up that overlooks miles and miles of fields."

"I guess that will be alright. I didn't see anyone following us. That's a good choice for a painting. I'll be by to check on you after I make a couple of phone calls."

With the fear subsided for now, she graced him with a coy grin. "Tell me who you're calling."

"I'd rather not. If my plan doesn't work, I'll need to come up with Plan B."

She tilted her head as a sign his response made no sense.

He spoke again before she could. "You're behind in making sketches. Get to work. I want us to both be at Katy House by five."

Her window drifted upward as she eased away from him. Fen went back to his truck and placed his first call to Deputy Cory Blane, Bailey's romantic interest. Actually, he was fully hooked on her, but because he worked long nights and caught extra shifts when he could their relationship was still in the fledgling stage. Fen had to hand it to him, there was no shortage of ambition with the young man.

A groggy voice answered after five rings. "Yeah."

"Cory, this is Fen."

The cracked voice told Fen he'd woken Cory from a deep sleep. "Sheriff Maguire? What time is it?"

"Early afternoon."

"Oh. What's wrong? Is it Bailey?"

"Before I tell you, stand up and get some blood flowing to your brain."

Only a couple of seconds passed before Cory announced, "I'm up. What happened to Bailey?"

"Nothing too bad yet, but I want your help to make sure it doesn't." He explained how Sonny had threatened and assaulted Bailey. Fen could almost hear Cory's teeth grind.

"I'm coming to get her. If you don't have enough evidence to have this Sonny character arrested, I'll make something up."

"I have a better idea. I'm calling Sheriff Rhoads to ask if he'll let me borrow you for a special protection detail. If he agrees, you won't have to use vacation days or take off without permission."

"I know the sheriff owes you a big favor for solving the cold case back in the spring, but my supervisors always complain about staffing. If he won't let me off, I'll turn in my badge."

"I know you would, but I don't think that will be necessary."

By the tenor and speed of his words, Cory was fully awake and thinking. "It's a good thing it's a B&B. I can sleep on a couch."

"It's better than that. Bailey and Ren are staying in two separate buildings in the backyard. There's a third apartment available for you. You'll stay right below Bailey. All she has to do is drop something heavy on the floor or scream."

"I'll pack for several days and come right away." The unmistakable sound of concern etched Cory's next words. "Is this guy really serious about getting to Bailey?"

"She demanded a pistol."

"That's not like her. She may be small, but she's fearless."

"Not with this guy. I'll call you back after I talk to Stony."

"Like I said, I'll turn in my badge if he doesn't agree to your request. Should I bring an extra pistol for Bailey?"

"Me, you, Thelma, and a local guy will be enough armed protection."

"Who's the other guy?"

"His name is John West. He's a city cop about your age who's taken a shine to Ren. I'll talk to him about making frequent patrols of the B&B. I believe he'll want to spend time with Ren when he's not working."

That Ren had attracted the attention of a young man didn't seem to surprise Cory. "Is John as quiet as Ren is talkative?"

Fen grinned. "Their relationship is only a day old, but they seem to confirm the theory that opposites attract."

A brief salutation ended one conversation and set the groundwork for a second phone call. By the tone of his voice, Fen caught the sheriff of Williamson County in a good mood.

After the preliminaries, Fen explained the reason for his call. The sheriff responded without hesitation. "Cory's yours for the rest of the week. Working with you again will do him good. It sounds like you're setting a trap to catch this Sonny Eastham."

"Only if he tries to get to Bailey."

"Be careful. I'm looking at Sonny's criminal history."

Two phone calls down, both with excellent results. Fen called Cory back and gave him the combination to the door locks in case Thelma wasn't home.

When Fen said Thelma's name, it occurred to him she needed to know about the additional mouth to feed and that Cory was staying in the apartment below Bailey.

The sound of traffic accompanied Thelma's voice.

"Where are you going?" asked Fen.

"To the dentist. Don't you remember?"

"My mind's been on other things."

"Like what?"

"Keeping Bailey safe."

The sound of squealing tires sounded through the phone, followed by Thelma shouting, "Go around!"

Fen waited a few more seconds before he heard, "I'm parked. What's Bailey done now?"

"Nothing, but Riley Eastham's son came to the park and did plenty."

"Like what?"

"Things that shouldn't happen to any woman. I'll let Bailey give you the details."

Thelma was rarely at a loss for words, but the prospect of Bailey being harmed struck her dumb. Her momentary silence gave Fen a chance to further explain. "The short-and-sweet is that Sonny Eastham came to the river to tell Bonnie Sterling she needed to get home and cook Riley's lunch. Bonnie left and Sonny stayed. It could have been much worse for Bailey, but a man who'd been fishing came along in time. The pistol in his shoulder holster hurried Sonny on his way."

Thelma took in the information. "I'm surprised Bailey didn't rearrange his underwear with a swift kick."

"He was too close. The way she described it, he had her pinned up against the rail. He scared her, and you know she doesn't scare easily. It wouldn't surprise me if he showed up sometime late at night in the next few days."

"What makes you say that?" demanded Thelma.

"He told her he would."

"That's all I need to know. Bailey's moving into my room and I'm sleeping on the couch. If that weasel thinks he's getting our girl, he'll learn a two-shot lesson."

"I've already taken care of things. She and Ren will stay where they are. Cory Blane is on his way to Smithville. He'll stay in the apartment below Bailey. I'm adding him to the roster of students. His assignment is to stay glued to Bailey any time she's out of her room. You'll need to cook for one more."

Thelma huffed. "I won't be able to sleep a wink knowing someone's stalking Bailey. I still like my idea of having her move into the main house."

"I want to send the low life back to prison. He won't chance coming into the main house, but I believe he's dumb enough to try to get into her apartment."

"I'd rather shoot him or call Sam to take care of him. They'd never find the body."

"It's tempting," said Fen, "but that's not the way I do things. As far as you shooting him, you'd probably miss with that dinky thing you're carrying."

Thelma released a sigh. "I don't like it, but I can see how having a lawman watching out for her is the smart thing to do." She paused. "How many bullets does that gun on his hip hold?"

"Fourteen before he has to put in a second clip."

"That should do the trick. If not, I'll put two more in him."

Fen needed to get back to being an art instructor but he had one more question for Thelma. "Are you going to meet with the lady who knows all there is to know about Smithville?"

"I did that this morning. Like I said, I'm on my way to the dentist's office."

"Ah. I forgot about you getting the crown back on. How do you question a dentist when he's digging around in your mouth?"

"I don't plan on it. The woman I spoke with this morning already told me about Dr. Fox." She took a breath. "I'm about to be late for my appointment and this tooth needs to be taken care of. It lets me know if I drink anything hot or cold. You and Bailey get home at a decent hour and we'll have a chin wag over supper."

Fen drove by to check on Bailey; all was quiet. He didn't want to draw too much attention to her, so he started his consultations with the artists who chose to paint the lake scene at the park. One by one he questioned the students on their choice of landscapes and how they intended to paint them. He also looked at the photos he told them to take every hour. It should have been an easy assignment, but many forgot to set a timer on their phone to remind them. He fully understood. Once he started sketching, time lost meaning.

He eventually joined Bailey and two other artists who chose to paint the most challenging scene, a panoramic view of fields. The other two sought shelter under a spindly tree that offered sparse shade. Fen spoke with them before moving to a folding chair with a golf umbrella attached.

Bailey looked up from her sketch pad. "Did you come up with a plan?"

"I did. Do you remember Sheriff Rhoads from Williamson County?"

"How could I forget?"

"He loaned Cory to me for the rest of the week." Her eyes widened and her mouth hinged open. No words came, so he continued. "He'll stay in the apartment below you. I told Thelma to cook for one more."

Bailey sprang to her feet and wrapped him in a hug before he knew what hit him. She eventually pulled away. "What will Cory do during the day?"

Fen chuckled. "He's going to learn to paint. Do you think there's room for one more under this umbrella, or do you want me to assign him to one of the other locations?"

"Don't even think about it."

He looked at the rolling hills that stretched in front of him. "You picked a glorious spot. I'm tempted to start sketching."

Bailey had other things on her mind. "When will Cory arrive?"

"He'll get to listen to Thelma for about two hours before we get home."

"Can I leave early?"

Fen shook his head. "You'll have to rush to finish by Saturday morning."

She wiggled her eyebrows. "No problem."

Fen glanced over his shoulder at the two other artists. "Those two need extra coaching, and this view is too good to waste. I'll set up beside them and sketch until you leave. Sonny doesn't know where you are, but I'm not taking any chances."

He used the time repositioning his truck to review his team's activities. Lou was at the courthouse in Bastrop looking into people's history and public records. Thelma spent a good portion of her morning talking to a woman who probably knew more about the city and its residents than anyone else in town. He didn't expect to learn much about the town's dentist, but Thelma said she had some things to share about him. Bailey had information and opinions about Riley Eastham and Bonnie Sterling. He would hear about those over supper. Ren spent the day painting a mural. He wondered what she might have learned. His gut told him that John somehow managed to fit his schedule around lunch with her. It could be interesting to talk to him, too.

He took slow steps toward the two artists. So far, his contribution to the pool of information had come from the city attorney. Audrey's openness about her past, including a son with a big secret, surprised him. Once again, he pondered why she was so open.

Fen realized he stood at a crossroads with Audrey. Should he trust her enough to share the information he was gathering and see what she could add to it, or continue to play his cards close to his vest?

He'd sleep on that last item until Lou did a more thorough check on her story about John's birth father. He stopped. No, he'd call Chuck and Candy. Somehow, Candy could find out about things that eluded Lou.

With all the fishing for information done today, they should catch something. He walked on. It promised to be an interesting talk around the supper table.

Chapter Sixteen

Lou expelled a full breath from puffed-out cheeks as she took a seat at the far end of the long dining room table. Fen looked at her from his seat at the other end. "Did you get lost on the way back to Smithville?"

She shook her head. "It was a busy day and I stopped at Buc-ee's in Bastrop, filled up my car with gas, and scored a large iced tea. There must be fifty or sixty gas pumps at that over-sized convenience store."

Ren added, "They have the best bathrooms on the planet. Almost as many stalls as there are gas pumps and they keep them clean."

Fen changed the subject. "Did you find anything interesting at the courthouse?"

Thelma's voice came from the kitchen. "No business talk until someone goes for seconds. I worked too hard on this meal for any of you to let it get cold." The swinging doors parted and Thelma arrived with two large platters of pot roast. She placed them on each end of the table and soon returned with twin bowls of roasted potatoes, onions, and carrots.

The cook extraordinaire announced, "Biscuits and gravy are on the way. There are three kinds of dressing for your salads."

Cory expressed his opinion. "Real food! I may have to kiss the cook."

"Don't try it," said Bailey. "She's handy with a knife."

Thelma gave Cory a hard look. "You heard her. No kissin'."

Chuckles sounded from several as Lou took a portion of meat and pushed the platter toward Ren. Despite Thelma's earlier command, silence wasn't the young artist's strong suit. "I had a great day painting and everyone I met seemed friendly except a guy who came by this afternoon. I think he'd been drinking or smoking weed." Her eyebrows narrowed. "He might have been high on something else. It was hard for me to tell because I was up near the top on a ladder. Anyway, he said some things that weren't nice. I ignored him and pretended I was deaf."

"Did it work?" asked Bailey.

She shrugged as she stabbed a chunk of potato with a fork. "When I looked down, he was driving off."

"What kind of vehicle?" asked Fen.

She spoke around the potato. "A new pickup." More details came after she chewed and swallowed. "It was fire-engine red and too fancy to be a work truck."

Bailey stiffened. "Was it lifted, with loud pipes?"

Ren had stuffed her mouth again and could only say, "Uh-huh."

Cory must have read Bailey's body language. "Is that the guy?"

She nodded.

"Who?" asked Lou.

Bailey found her voice. "Sonny Eastham." She turned to look at Ren. "Stay away from him. He's bad news."

Lou added, "That's the gospel truth. I took a reporter from Bastrop to lunch today. She had plenty to say about Sonny, and none of it was good. His dad and future stepmom seem all right, but Sonny is a different story."

Thelma returned from the kitchen and put two bowls of biscuits wrapped in dish towels on the table. "These are hot, but they won't be for long if you talk instead of eating."

The conversation fell off until Fen pushed his plate a couple of inches away from him. Thelma looked up and tilted her head. "What's wrong with you tonight?"

"Nothing. The meal was wonderful. You know I slack up on eating when there's a lot to think about. Tell us what you discovered about Smithville today."

Thelma put her fork down. "Like most small towns, it has its fair share of people doing things they shouldn't, but there's mostly good folk living here."

"Who holds the most power and influence?" asked Lou.

"Mildred Fox, but she's in her mid-eighties. It won't be long before there's going to be a power struggle."

"Between who?" asked Lou.

"Her son, the dentist, and Riley Eastham."

Fen broke in. "What was your impression of Dr. Fox?"

Thelma scratched her ear. "My tooth doesn't hurt, so I guess he's all right as a dentist. As a man, my new friend called him a momma's boy. She thinks big changes are coming to Smithville." Thelma ran her hand down her glass. "He reminded me of weak, unsweetened, caffeine-free tea. It's all right, but not much to it."

Fen turned to Lou. "Did you find out anything else about Dr. Fox?"

"Born and raised in Smithville. He went on to college and married after he finished dental school. No children. Wife died of cancer. Otherwise, he's led a squeaky-clean life. He lives with his mother and owns a ranch outside of town."

Bailey added her opinion. "He sounds boring to me. I'm not sure what to make of Riley Eastham. Bonnie Sterling talked about him like he walks on water."

"Not everyone shares that opinion," said Lou. "His name is on a small collection of civil lawsuits. He wins most that go to trial, which isn't many."

"Why is that?" asked Bailey.

Fen explained. "Money buys talented attorneys. It also allows businesses to settle for smaller amounts." He looked at Lou. "How many companies does he own?"

"Plenty. He plays offense."

Ren asked, "Why does anyone do business with him?"

Thelma had the answer. "I learned that most of the old timers don't. It's the move-ins that like his fast-paced way of doing things. There's talk he wants to put in a business park and new subdivision on the loop around town, but he can't get his hands on the property."

Cory reached for seconds and asked. "I'm confused. What does any of this have to do with the guy who was murdered and dumped in the river?"

Fen leaned back. "That's the best question I've heard yet. I'm working on something that's probably a long shot." He turned to Lou. "Did you find out anything else about the victim, Lee Grimes?"

"My reporter contact couldn't add anything to what we already know about him. He was an enigma. Great at coming up with unique crimes, but totally inept at committing them." She paused. "What have you been holding back?"

"Ben told me Grimes made phone calls to people that the cops either couldn't, or didn't, follow up on. It's like they stopped looking after they arrested Riley. I hate loose ends like that."

"What do you want me to do about it?"

"I noticed some went to a number in Dallas. I called Candy this morning and asked her to run a check on who received the calls. It's a business in Bonnie Sterling's name."

Fen became quiet for several seconds as the people around the table stared at him. "Lou, your assignment is Riley Eastham. Go to Dallas tomorrow and do whatever it takes to discover if his alibi checks out."

Lou was a stickler for details. "You said some of Lee Grimes's calls went to Dallas. What about the others?"

"He called a lot of people. Candy's double-checking phone records."

Bailey asked, "Didn't the local cops do that?"

"They stopped looking after Riley was arrested." Fen cleared his throat. "Sometimes it's wise to use outside people."

"That means you don't trust them."

"Let's just say they've had plenty of time to do something so obvious."

"There's always a motive for killing someone," said Lou. "If we can find out who Lee called in the time leading up to his murder, I bet we'll open up a can of worms." She rubbed her hands together. "This case is shaping up better than I thought it would."

Fen's words of warning came next. "Let's not forget that the only persons we're looking for are those that had something to do with killing Lee Grimes. We're not here to destroy reputations."

Cory changed the mood at the table when a burp made an untimely escape. He dipped his head. "Excuse me."

Thelma grinned. "Sam says that's the way Choctaw Indians

tell a cook they liked the meal. There may be hope for you yet." She paused. "Now, just because I said that don't give you any kind of license with me, young man. If you get it in your mind to climb the stairs to Bailey's room, you and I will have a short, loud talk."

Bailey rolled her eyes and turned to Fen. "Do you hear what I have to put up with? The more I think about it, the more I'm ready to start college in Georgetown next January."

Thelma stood and gathered three plates to take to the kitchen. "I can't stop you, but I don't have to send cookies with you."

Fen jumped into the fray before it got loud. "Speaking of cookies. What's for dessert?"

"Whatever they'll make you at the Dairy Queen. That dentist was slow as a lame mule. You're lucky I put the roast in before I left."

The ringing of the doorbell put an end to the conversation. Fen rose as the others ferried dishes to the kitchen. He glanced through a window but only saw the back of a head with black hair arranged in a bun at the base of a woman's neck. She turned when the sound of the door opening alerted her. Green eyes met his stare.

"Hello, Sheriff. I hear you have company."

Fen tried to make a quick recovery. This was the third time he'd seen Audrey and she'd dressed differently on each occasion. Today's pinstriped business jacket was form-fitting with an equally snug matching skirt. He couldn't help but admire how she filled them out.

He stepped back and gave her what he hoped wasn't too wide of a smile. "Come in, counselor. You're dressed for business. I hope you haven't come to serve me with a subpoena."

She shot him a sideways glance. "Have you been naughty?"

He coughed and stood up straight. "I've been innocent as an altar boy."

"I knew an altar boy when I was in the ninth grade. He tried to get me drunk on stolen communion wine, so that statement doesn't reassure me."

She continued without missing a beat. "You and your art students are the talk of the town. The way I hear it, all the women want you to spend more time giving them personal instruction."

Fen wondered how she managed to stuff so many sentences with dual meanings. It stroked his ego but left him uncomfortable at the same time. Time to get on firmer ground. "Would you like to meet the other guests?"

She gave him a look that said, *Who do you think you're fooling?* She blinked twice and said, "I'd love to meet your crew of crime solvers."

Fen narrowed his eyes, not admitting, or denying, anything.

She blinked and leaned closer. "It's our secret. I put it together after speaking with Ben's wife. I'm taking belly dancing classes with her." She sighed. "It's a class full of lonely wives and fellow spinsters."

Fen fought off the mental image of Audrey shaking and ching-ching-a-linging. "Ben's wife is a wonderful woman, but my wife, Sally, shared something personal with her once." He paused. "Only once."

Audrey put her hand on his arm. "I've not told a soul why you're here and I'm not going to."

Fen had two choices. He could ask her to leave or go ahead and introduce her to the crew. He chose the latter, but not before another knock sounded on the door. Ren, Bailey, and Cory appeared in the living room. Ren buzzed past Fen and Audrey standing in the entry but spoke as she did so. "Hi. I'm Ren. That's John at the door."

She threw the door open, took John's hand, and pulled him

into the home. John came to a sudden stop. "Mom? What are you doing here?"

Audrey raised perfectly sculpted eyebrows. "I was going to ask you the same question."

"This is Ren. We're going to get ice cream."

Chapter Seventeen

I t was one of those awkward moments when no one spoke for several seconds. For the first time since Fen met Audrey, she was at a loss for words. He took pity on her and continued the introductions. "Audrey West, this is Bailey Madison and her boyfriend, Cory Blane. Bailey is what you might call my protégé. She has a small apartment and studio above my garage."

Audrey extended a hand for Bailey to shake and followed that with nodding a greeting to Ren. "My goodness. Two lovely young ladies and two handsome officers of the law."

Fen paid particular attention to Audrey. He wondered how she would react to her son's probing question about why his mother was at a bed-and-breakfast speaking to a former sheriff. He had to hand it to Audrey; she proved to be quick on her feet. She cast her gaze to Ren. "Are you also one of Sheriff Maguire's students?"

"Yes and no. Fen's the best teacher in the world. He knows everything there is about painting. I specialize in large murals.

In fact, I'm redoing the one on the building across the street. It was a shame to let it get so faded."

Ren snapped her fingers. "John says you're the city attorney. You must know every building in town and who owns them. Are there any more that could stand sprucing up or anyone who would like a mural? It's common for city governments to want murals depicting important historic events. Does Smithville have a line item in their budget for that?"

Ren's words came to a sudden stop and she lowered her head. "Sorry. My dad says I have a mouth like a shot glass in a downpour. It's always running over. I talked so little to anyone today that my words are sloshing out even more than usual."

Audrey shifted her gaze to John and then back to Ren. "Young lady, don't change. The world needs talkers to counter the silence from people like my son."

"Hey. That's not fair. I talk when I have something to say."

Cory gave Audrey a questioning look. "How did you know I'm a cop?"

She pointed to Cory's right hip. "If you want to get rid of the bulge, try a pancake holster. An off-duty pistol with a smaller frame and less capacity would also help." She turned to Fen. "Is that what you're wearing?"

He gave a nod and lifted the un-tucked tail of his shirt. "I hardly know it's there."

Fen turned to face Bailey. "Did I hear something about you four going for ice cream? If it were me, I'd leave before two old people tagged along."

Bailey wasted no time. "Whose truck are we taking?"

"Mine's the closest," said Cory.

The foursome blew out the front door as if carried along by a summer dust-devil. Audrey turned to Fen. "I feel old."

"You don't look it." He bit the inside of his lip as Audrey searched his eyes.

"Thank you, Sheriff."

He turned from her gaze and changed the subject. "There are two more people you need to meet." He heard footsteps scurrying toward the dining room, followed by the sound of the kitchen door swinging shut. Lou was standing at the coffee service when he and Audrey went through the living room and into the dining room.

He introduced the newspaper reporter to the attorney, and the two exchanged words of mutual respect. Written between the lines was the fact that they both already knew much about each other.

Fen didn't speak again until the two agreed to meet sometime that week and have a proper conversation. This didn't surprise him in the least. Lou was always digging for details, and it seemed Audrey was cut from the same cloth.

"Thelma?" said Fen in a voice loud enough to carry beyond the dining room. "Can you hear all right in there, or do I need to come in and introduce you to Audrey?"

"I'm busy cleaning up the mess from supper. I didn't hear anyone volunteering to help."

He jerked his head to one side as a signal for him and Audrey to make their escape. Lou said, "Run along while you have a chance. I'm going upstairs to watch the national news."

Fen led the way to the front door and didn't speak until they were on the porch. "Let's sit and you can tell me why you came tonight. Thelma will come out and offer you something to drink. Then she'll ask you a few leading questions. If you don't want company, give her one-word answers."

Audrey looked at the row of rocking chairs. "She's a good bodyguard."

"Sometimes too good."

Audrey settled into a rocker halfway down the porch. Fen parked himself next to her. Cicadas provided the soundtrack for the late-summer night. Creaks and squeaks sounded as the two chairs got into a rhythm.

Fen broke the silence. "Something's bothering me about the case."

"Only one thing?"

"One thing at a time. The knife that was used to kill Lee Grimes. Why didn't the person who killed him throw it in the river or dispose of it someplace else?"

"I wondered the same thing. What are your theories?"

"Let's turn the calendar back further than when the murder took place. What if Riley Eastham lost his knife before the killing?"

"That's a big if."

"Agreed, but I think his attorneys have an ace up their sleeve that they won't play until the civil suit against the city goes to trial."

Audrey stopped rocking. "Are you forgetting that Riley was in Dallas at the time of the murder?"

Fen didn't answer. The rocking continued until Audrey stopped and said, "Holy smoke. You think he fabricated his alibi. I didn't consider that possibility. He's a crafty business-man, but killing isn't his style." Her full lips pinched into a narrow line. "Now you have me wondering if I've misjudged Riley."

Excitement seasoned her words. "I never thought of going back any farther than the murder. He didn't report the knife lost or stolen."

Fen sighed. "It's only a theory." He cast his gaze her way and looked longer than necessary at the spot where her skirt ended and the thigh below it shone in the streetlight. A clearing of his throat and averting his eyes wasn't enough to erase the image.

To regain his equilibrium, he changed the subject. "Earlier, I asked why you came here tonight."

Audrey uncrossed her legs and pulled her skirt down to a less revealing length. "I came to talk to you about John and Ren."

"What about them?"

"I heard John was seeing some new girl in town, so I came to see if I should be worried. John wants to spend a year in law enforcement before he goes to law school. He's already taken the LSAT and aced it. What he lacks is confidence in himself and getting tougher."

Fen took a stab at what he believed was Audrey's true motive. "You want to make sure he doesn't trade long-range plans for short-term pleasures."

Audrey lifted her chin. "That was indelicate, but you hit the nail on the head."

"I'm sorry. It was judgmental." He took a breath. "You hit a sore spot with me. Thelma and I have an ongoing battle about how to release Bailey into a dangerous world filled with temptations. She had to endure unwanted advances from Sonny Eastham today."

Both chairs stopped rocking. "Give me details," said Audrey.

Fen did and ended with, "That's why Cory is staying in the apartment under Bailey's for the rest of the week."

"Does John know about the assault?"

"My guess is the four of them are discussing it over milkshakes while we sit in these rockers."

A glimmer of revelation shone in Audrey's eyes. "That explains why you have a pistol on your hip. You're setting a trap for Sonny to fall into."

"Most bullies are cowards, but if he comes for her, we're ready."

The front door opened, and Thelma made her appearance carrying two glasses. "I made fresh-squeezed lemonade." She handed a glass to Fen first and then gave one to Audrey. "How are things at city hall?"

"Fine."

"I hear you're quite the cowgirl. Did you grow up on a ranch?"

"Sort of."

"Was it nearby?"

"No."

Fen interrupted. "Thelma, are you sure there aren't any cookies? You know how I love cookies with lemonade. The sweet and tart make my taste buds happy."

"Me, too," said Audrey.

A huff followed. "The only ingredients I have are for peanut butter cookies. That means I'll have to mess up the kitchen and they won't be ready for an hour."

Fen challenged her. "Twenty minutes tops. I like mine chewy."

"Hot, chewy cookies are my favorites," said Audrey. "I don't care what they are."

Thelma turned on a heel. "Don't blame me if they give you gas. Eating raw cookies is a good way to get sick."

The door slammed shut. Audrey chuckled. "I can tell you two like sparring."

Fen didn't deny it but said, "We have about ten minutes before she'll be back to refill our glasses."

"Can you put my mind at ease concerning John and Ren?"

Chapter Eighteen

Fen had to arrange his thoughts. How could he describe a young woman like Ren Duvant? He pulled in a full breath. "Ren's father is a free-spirited musician in Austin."

Audrey scowled. "If that's supposed to make me not worry, you're failing."

"Her mother works for the IRS."

"That's marginally better."

"Her grandfather Duvant is the largest landowner in Williamson County. His ranch dwarfs mine, plus he has other business interests."

"Interesting, but it doesn't tell me anything about Ren."

Fen pointed to the building across the street. "You can't see it very well, but Ren spent all day climbing up and down a ladder repainting that mural. She's paying for the paint out of her own pocket. I'll try to reimburse her, but she won't accept it."

He took in another breath. "Ren's one of a kind and is thoroughly in love with life. Never met a stranger. I liken her to a pretty butterfly. She flits from one spot to the next."

Audrey pushed out her lips. "She doesn't sound very stable."

Fen's eyebrows lifted to signal a question. "Isn't that what you want? Someone who's not going to be around John long?"

"I'm not sure what kind of girl I want for John, but one that's flighty and immature certainly isn't it."

"You're misunderstanding what I'm trying to say. There's too much difference between her and John. Ren's a twelve-year-old wrapped in a woman's body. She makes friends and isn't interested in long-term relationships. I don't think she'll be ready for any type of romantic relationship for the next five years. She'll have her work done and leave by Sunday morning if we've finished the case or not."

Fen took in another breath. "John has a full-time job. He's also helping us catch Sonny Eastham if he comes for Bailey. He might squeeze in a few double dates, but Ren's more interested in repainting a mural than she is in John. If she finishes the mural early, I'll keep her busy working on a portrait she started."

"I may look around for another faded mural to make sure she has plenty to keep her busy."

Audrey pushed up on the arms of the rocker. Fen did the same. "You're a deep thinker, Sheriff Maguire."

Fen wondered what would come next. A hug? Perhaps a kiss? Audrey's extended hand answered the question. "Good night," she said. A sparkle of mischief came into her eyes. "Do you want Thelma to keep guessing about us?"

He gave his head a nod. "She loves to pull my chain. Let's keep her on her toes for the rest of the week."

"This could be fun."

Fen noticed Thelma move to the window behind them. He cut his eyes toward the interloper, but only after turning so only Audrey could see his signal. Then he raised his voice. "And you, Audrey, are a very beautiful woman. Do you mind if I kiss you goodnight?"

A gasp sounded through the single-pane window, followed by footfalls. They both had to turn toward the street to redirect their muffled spurts of laughter.

Fen walked Audrey to her truck. All thoughts of an aborted kiss fled when something else popped into his mind. "There's something that's been bugging me about the case."

She stopped on the sidewalk and wagged her head. "That's the fastest one-hundred-and-eighty turn in a conversation I've experienced. Please tell me you never did that to your wife."

Fen dipped his head. "I needed to get back on solid ground. Besides, it's a question that you might know the answer to."

Eyebrows raised in question, she waited for him to continue.

"Lou's going to Dallas to verify Riley's alibi. If he didn't kill Grimes, then what would be so important to him that he would lie about it?"

Audrey looked away, then brought her gaze back to him. "I don't have an answer to that question."

"If he did come back to Smithville and killed Grimes, why?"

She shrugged. "All I know is, if Lou can find evidence that Riley wasn't in Dallas, he's back in the frame for murder."

Fen shook his head. "But why?"

"Why what?"

"What motive could Riley have for killing a mostly incompetent criminal?"

"That's the type of thing detectives discover for attorneys. If you want me to guess, I'd say Lee Grimes discovered something big about Riley and tried to blackmail him."

Fen nodded his head in agreement. "I thought the same thing."

Audrey opened the door to her truck, but didn't climb in. "Riley carries a lockblade knife in a brown leather scabbard. He's on the city council so I see him at the meetings, plus I occasionally run into him around town. I've never seen him without a knife on his hip unless he's wearing slacks."

Fen watched as Audrey turned the corner, then returned to the white chair on the porch. The longer he rocked, the more convinced he became that the day was a success. Bailey was under round-the-clock protection now. That was his biggest relief. He'd also learned a lot about the city from Thelma and Audrey. Lou would leave in the morning for Dallas. There was still much to be done, but his sense of satisfaction meant he would have a better night's sleep even if Thelma didn't.

Fen stopped rocking as something occurred to him. He'd learned very little about Riley from Bailey's time spent with Bonnie Sterling. He decided a more direct approach could yield better results. He had two options: Talk to Bonnie or go directly to Riley.

Fen pulled out his phone and called Bailey. "How's the ice cream?"

"Cold and yummy. What's up?"

"A quick question. Did you get anything useful out of Bonnie today?"

"Not much. I was saving the probing questions for this afternoon."

"Do you think she'll return to the river tomorrow?"

"She said she would. Riley has meetings in Austin tomorrow. I learned that much."

"I'll call her and say I'm starting my day at the river."

"Do you want me and Cory to come there?"

"Go back to where you were today. I'll tell her the river didn't inspire you to produce a painting that told a good story."

"It inspired me to paint a homicide."

"Let's stick with peaceful landscapes. They sell better."

Bailey ended the conversation with, "Ren's making a racket by slurping the last of her milkshake through a straw. We'd better get out of here before we're asked to leave."

"Keep your eye out for you-know-who."

"You don't have to worry about that. Both cops have their heads on swivels."

The call ended and Fen rose to go to his room to retrieve the class roster that included phone numbers. Pans banged and clanged from the direction of the kitchen. He concluded Thelma needed to blow off steam, so he took a hard left in the entryway and climbed the stairs. He'd leave her to it.

A few minutes later, he punched in Bonnie's phone number. "Hello, Bonnie. This is Fen Maguire. I'm sorry I didn't get to spend any time with you today. I hope to make it up to you by coming to the river first thing tomorrow morning. Will you be there?"

"Oh, yes. I'd forgotten to do something at home and had to leave, but only for about an hour. I came back and did everything you said. You were right about how the light changes the mood. I'm having a bit of trouble deciding if I want the excitement of an early morning or the more muted evening shadows."

"If you had more time, you could do multiple paintings and tell several stories."

She gasped. "I never considered that. I won't have time to complete more than one in the time remaining, but that's a wonderful idea for future works."

"We'll talk about it more tomorrow morning. I should be there around nine."

"I'm free all day tomorrow and hope to catch the sunrise through the trees."

The buoyancy in her voice surprised him. He had Riley pegged as an overbearing, perhaps violent, partner to Bonnie. It occurred to him that Riley and his son were two unique people. Even a good tree could produce rotten fruit.

It still wasn't late and Audrey's snappy conversation had stimulated his mind, so Fen made three trips to his truck retrieving a painter's canvas, along with brushes, paints, and an easel. That left only the unfinished painting of the two generations of tractors to bring upstairs. It was time to paint and think.

To tell the story, he'd spend the rest of the week adding the old tractor as it chugged off the canvas into retirement. One generation gone and a new one to replace it. He imagined what the next generation of tractors might look like, but it was too much for the story. That existed somewhere in the future, over the plowed hill, on another painting.

After an hour's work, he cleaned his brushes and prepared for bed. After turning off the light, he chuckled as the streetlight cast shadows on the ceiling. Thelma's proclivity to snoop into other's lives had come back to bite her. He'd do anything for her, but he didn't appreciate her stepping over invisible boundary lines. It was her turn to have a sleepless night. He'd need to get up in time to make sure she didn't alienate any of the others because she was angry with him.

Chapter Nineteen

The weather was still cooperating with the class schedule for painting, but rain was in the forecast for the next day. Fen glanced out the window and saw nothing but a tiny portion of a small, sleepy town. He showered, shaved, and dressed for the day.

As expected, Thelma was already banging and clanging in the kitchen. He whistled a jaunty tune as he entered the dining room.

"Keep that racket down," said Thelma, even though the noise she generated surpassed his.

He ignored her command and spoke in a normal voice. "Is the coffee ready, or do I need to use the single-serve?"

She came out of the kitchen with a full carafe. "This is real coffee. Those girls are bound to need a jolt of something to get them awake. Are you going to wake them and that boy from Georgetown?"

"He's not a boy, and I hadn't planned on it. Did they get in late?"

"How should I know?"

Fen put a serious tone in his voice. "What time?"

"It was almost eleven."

He put another layer of strength to his words. "What time?"

She huffed a quick reply. "Five after ten."

"Any sign of a new, red pickup truck driving slowly past the property?"

"Not that I remember, but there were plenty of others. That road stays busy until the bars close. Between the cars, trucks, and those blasted trains, it's a wonder this town isn't the insomnia capital of Texas."

Lou breezed into the dining room, fully dressed and with a spring in her step. "What a great mattress and pillow. I can't remember the last time I had such a good night's sleep."

Thelma released a huff of air through her nose. "You'll have to wait a while for breakfast. I wasn't expecting you up so early."

"Only coffee for me this morning. I'll stop in Elgin. There's a donut shop on this side of town and a food trailer on the other side that sells breakfast tacos. I may get both."

Thelma pointed at the single serve. "If you're going to poison yourself, you might as well go all the way." She spun around and went into the kitchen.

Lou whispered. "What's wrong with her?"

Fen rose and whispered for Lou to follow him. He picked up the overnight bag that she'd left by the stairs and carried it out the front door before explaining Thelma's short fuse. "She's going through a combination of sleep deprivation and sensory overload. This is unfamiliar territory, and she doesn't have enough eyes, ears, or energy to keep up with all that's going on. Maybe one less person to care for will help Thelma settle down. Plus it's important we verify Riley's alibi, and you'll avoid the inevitable confrontation I'll need to have."

"With whom?"

"We won't know until you report your findings."

"That's an interesting response. Evasive, but interesting. What did you learn from Audrey last night?"

"She's very protective of her son—afraid he and Ren might be up to something that would torpedo his future."

Lou had a nose for news, which meant she had a sixth sense concerning trouble, or lack of it. "That won't happen for several reasons. The primary one is you have Thelma watching her day and night. Bailey and Cory are doing the same."

Lou pressed the key fob to unlock her car. Fen opened a back door and pitched her bag in. "Can you make it to Bastrop without coffee? It's only five-thirty and I'm not sure anything around here is open this early."

"It may be difficult, but I'll make it. See you in a couple of days."

"Be safe," said Fen.

"Same to you. I'll expect a full report when I get back."

"I hope there's something to tell you."

Lou spoke with absolute confidence and threw in a grin for good measure. "You have a habit of stirring pots until something rises to the surface. Something interesting will happen by the time I get back."

Fen returned to the dining room, settled into the chair at the head of the table, and took a sip of coffee. It was somewhere between warm and the temperature he preferred. He grabbed the carafe and added two inches of steaming stimulant.

It wasn't long before Thelma pulled out the chair to his left and plopped into it. Companionable silence filled the room. He wondered what colors he'd mix to paint the dark circles under her eyes.

The liquid in his cup reached the halfway mark before he

broke the silence. "Do you know what I learned about sleeping when I was a state trooper and a sheriff?"

She yawned and shook her head.

"Sleep when you can."

Thelma examined her fingernails. "My mind won't let me."

Fen had known this was coming and wanted to help his overprotective cook. "I'll tell Bailey and Ren to eat something at the coffee shop today. I'll eat at the bakery."

She opened her mouth to say something, but his hand became a stop sign. "Listen to me." Only a second ticked by. "You're not home and Sam's not here watching over everything that goes on outside."

"Snakes crawl at night, even in a city. I'm worried sick that something will happen to those girls."

"That's why you need to sleep during the day and stay vigilant at night. Nothing will happen during the daytime except Sonny driving by in his truck. Part of his game is instilling fear. Cory has Bailey's blind side and John is taking care of Ren."

"He can't be with her all day."

"He doesn't need to. You spoke the truth when you said snakes roam at night. John has the daytime officers making regular patrols of where she's painting."

"How do you know that?"

"It's what I'd do." He took a breath. "Besides, Ren has the instincts of a squirrel. If she senses danger, she'll scurry up the ladder."

Thelma clasped her hands together. "You almost have me convinced, but not quite."

Fen cast his gaze to a window on the other side of the room, hoping for one more thing to convince Thelma she needed to sleep. It came in a flash of inspiration. "I'll trade trucks with you today. If, and when, Sonny drives by, he'll think I'm at home."

Thelma let her shoulders drop a quarter of an inch. "That might work for today, but what about tomorrow?"

He paused, but only for a second. "Cory will park his truck here. He and Bailey will ride together in her truck. The next day, it could be John's truck. It will keep Sonny guessing."

Her shoulders came down in a sign of surrender. "I guess I could sleep a little on the couch during the day."

Fen looked at his phone to check the time. "I'll have Cory walk with Bailey and Ren to the coffee shop while I go to the bakery. We'll all stay there until it's time to get to work."

"Sack lunches are in the refrigerator. Making them helped me stay awake between three and four this morning."

Fen ended the conversation with, "It's supposed to rain tomorrow. If it does, you can sleep all day. I'll tell everyone in the class to paint from home."

"What will Cory do?"

"Bailey's going to teach him to paint."

Fen rose, took the now cool half cup of coffee to the kitchen sink, and poured it out. He then went back through the dining room. Thelma was spreading a throw on the couch. "I thought you were leaving."

"I need to get my keys and wallet."

"Don't forget your pistol."

He patted his right hip. "And my pistol."

Thelma didn't stir as he placed the keys to his truck on the coffee table and picked up hers. He exited through the front door and followed the sidewalk around the house. Muted lights shone through the windows of two of the three apartments.

Instead of knocking on doors, he waited. Cory was the first to exit his room, but not before peeking out the window. Fen nodded his approval. The young man checked to make sure Sonny wasn't lurking in the shadows.

"Good morning," said Cory as he came to where Fen stood

under a light. "I heard Bailey come to life about thirty minutes ago. She should be down any time."

"I don't see a light on in Ren's apartment. She must have forgotten to set her alarm."

Cory looked up at the apartment in a separate building. "Doesn't surprise me. She claims clocks are evil and we should allow nature to order our days." He took a step toward the stairway leading up to Ren's apartment. "I'll get her."

It wasn't long before Cory had scaled the stairs and knocked on the door. He knocked again. Fen took steps toward the stairway after no light came on after the third knock.

A sinking sensation made the coffee sour in Fen's stomach. Bailey exited her door. "What's with all the banging?"

Cory answered. "Is Ren with you?"

Shaking her head, she said, "Punch in the code. It's the same as yours."

Chapter Twenty

Fen watched as Bailey ran down the stairs of her apartment, crossed the distance to the next stairway, and bolted upward, taking two steps at a time. Cory struggled to punch in the correct four numbers of the key code. The lock spun a few seconds before Bailey arrived.

Cory had his pistol in hand when he spoke a word of warning. "Stay back until I clear the room."

He pushed the door open but didn't immediately enter, choosing instead to stand on one side in a crouched position. When a shot didn't ring out, he reached inside and flicked on the light. No sounds came from the opening.

Bailey couldn't wait and tried to rush through the opening. Cory's outstretched arm brought her forward progress to an abrupt stop. Feet went skyward, and she landed with a thud on her rump. Cory ignored her for the time being and focused only on entering the room. It wasn't long before he announced. "All clear. Ren's not here."

By this time, Fen was peeking over the top stair. "Get out of there and don't touch anything."

Fen was back on ground level when he saw the back door to the main house swing open. Light preceded the figure of someone descending the steps. The person walked into the same light Fen had stood under in the middle of the yard.

"What's all the hollering about?" asked Ren, as she munched a cookie.

Fen stayed where he was, putting together the pieces of what had transpired.

Bailey used a more direct approach. "You goober! You scared us to death."

"Why?"

"We thought Sonny kidnapped you."

"No way. I pushed a chair under the doorknob and had my can of pepper spray on the nightstand all night."

Ren held out a napkin stuffed with cookies. "I hope Thelma doesn't mind that I found her stash. She must have made them last night."

A city patrol car pulled up to the curb and John exited. "Is everything all right?"

Ren jogged to him as he approached. "Want a cookie? They're super-yummy."

He refused the gift, at least for the time being. "Why are Fen and Cory holding their pistols?"

Ren shrugged. "Beats me."

Fen holstered his weapon and gave details of how he had gone out the front door at the same time Ren entered the kitchen through the back door.

John and Cory had a good laugh while Bailey rubbed her backside and Fen whispered a brief prayer of gratitude. The event reminded him how quickly bad things can happen.

"We'd better move this party to the coffee shop," said Fen. "I'd hate for us to disturb Thelma's sleep."

Ren's laugh carried the sound of birdsong. "No chance of that. I heard her snoring. She's down and out."

John used his patrol car to transport Ren the three blocks down the street. Bailey walked between Fen and Cory along the empty street.

"How are you holding up?" Fen asked Bailey.

"I'll be better when my heart slows down." She walked three more steps before speaking. "I noticed Lou's car was gone. When did she leave?"

"A half hour ago. I hope her time in Dallas is productive." He kicked a rock to the curb.

Bailey then asked, "Are you going to talk to Bonnie today?"

"She'll be my first stop. I called her yesterday and verified that Riley is going to be in meetings out of town all day."

A shiver coursed its way through Bailey. "That place by the river makes my skin crawl."

"What's your impression of Bonnie?"

"She's cool and doesn't mind talking. I wish I could have spent more time with her."

"What did you two talk about?"

"Mostly painting. She's trying to depict the river flowing. It's supposed to represent a washing away of old ideas and replacing them with something new. I think she got the inspiration when a log floated by." She paused. "It wasn't really a log, but a large branch. Her sketch showed a massive tree, minus the branches, with the roots still attached."

Cory added his opinion. "That sounds like she's using poetic license to depict something only hinted at by reality."

Fen looked over Bailey's head and focused on Cory. "That's very insightful. Perhaps she's optimistic about her fiancé bringing change to town. Works of art can tell you a lot about the artist."

Bailey had a different opinion. "All I saw was a muddy

river. I can't help but think about a kayak with a body trailing behind it. Mega-creepy."

Fen dropped the subject of the river and moved on to something new. "Cory, have you ever tried to draw or paint?"

"Some. I can draw a reasonable likeness of a cloud."

"That's a start. I'd like for you to try your hand at expressionism."

"Modern art?" asked Cory.

"That stuff's weird," said Bailey.

Fen ignored Bailey's comment. "In expressionism, the artist sacrifices reality for feelings. General outlines and bold strokes transfer colors that depict deep emotions."

Bailey picked up where Fen left off. "It's supposed to communicate some sort of emotional intensity. I like to experiment with it when I'm boiling mad. Otherwise, I'm more into what I call muted-photorealism."

"What in the world is that?"

Fen nodded his approval as Bailey explained. "It's something like an airbrushed photograph. There's good money in painting portraits, baskets of fruit, and other still-life objects. What people don't want to see are zits, wrinkles, sags, bags, or other imperfections. There's no doubt about who or what you're looking at, but you give nature a helping hand."

Fen added. "Back to expressionism. It's a difficult medium to master. You're a sensitive young man, even though you're a cop. I think you'll enjoy expressing how you feel without worrying about conventional thinking of what a painting should look like." He paused. "Besides, it beats standing around while Bailey concentrates then yells if she's interrupted. She can go for hours without saying a word."

The conversation ended at the door of the coffeehouse. "I'm going to the bakery and have my breakfast. See if you can engage someone in conversation. Find out if they think the town should stay like it is or try to modernize and expand."

Bailey looked back toward the bed-and-breakfast. "We'll find someone to talk to." She then brought her gaze back to Fen. "Thelma's not cooking today?"

"Stuff your face with whatever you like. You two are free to paint all day. Be as quiet as you can when you go back to get your truck. Sack lunches are in the refrigerator."

On the short walk to the bakery, Fen thought about what delicacy he'd have first. He'd wait to see what struck his fancy.

A few early risers had lined up at the counter, but the early morning rush didn't amount to much. He examined the selections and chose a sausage kolache and two glazed donuts. He added a cup of coffee but doubted he'd finish it. The brew wasn't bad, but it didn't hold a candle to what came out of the percolator at the B&B.

The morning passed with customers coming and going. Work, weather, and family were the primary topics of conversation from a trio of gray-haired men who sat at a nearby table. Fen was only a minute or two from leaving when an elderly lady and a man a generation younger than her came through the door. She held a cane in her right hand but seemed to resent having to use it. The cane went down with a resounding thwack with each step, calling attention to it, and herself.

The man with her walked a half-step behind, making her the center of attention, which she seemed to prefer.

The reaction of the people took Fen by surprise. A pair of slouching men corrected their posture. The employees stiffened. No one saluted, bowed, or curtsied, but it wouldn't have surprised him if they had.

"Good morning, Mrs. Fox," said the woman behind the counter. She shifted her gaze to the man. "Dr. Fox, how are you today?"

Mildred Fox didn't give her son the opportunity to speak. "We're tolerable. It's still too hot for my liking." She scanned the tables and chairs. "You could use a few more customers. Is anything wrong?"

"It's the normal mid-week traffic. You know. Slow, but steady. The art festival this weekend will more than make up for a light day or two. I've already received several large orders."

Fen inspected the woman. She didn't skimp on the quality of the clothes she wore. Nor did she go light on hairspray that anchored every strand of gray. Poised and proud, there was no doubt this was the matriarch of Smithville.

It sounded like a regal proclamation when she said. "Box up an assortment of two dozen pastries and give them to Clayton. I have a garden club meeting this morning and Willie Jane came down with another bout of gout yesterday. I'd let her go, but I'm such a sentimental old fool."

Clayton traded places with his mother as she turned and took a long look at Fen. The woman thumped her way toward him, so he stood.

"Are you the visiting artist?"

He nodded. "Fen Maguire."

"Mr. Maguire, I'm aware of your reputation. Audrey West speaks highly of your skill as an artist. That's rather unusual, considering your background in law enforcement."

"I try to please my customers and myself," said Fen.

"Many try. Few succeed." She looked out the window and brought her gaze back to him. "I'd like to speak with you more about the class you're conducting. How does sometime tomorrow sound?"

Fen didn't want to sound too anxious, so he said. "I'm committed to giving guidance to the artists from nine in the morning until four thirty in the afternoon."

"Inclement weather is moving in late tonight. How do you propose to teach outdoors in the rain?"

"I'm scheduling people to bring their works-in-progress to The Katy House at set times throughout the day. I find giving individual critiques and suggestions to be effective. After all, we want the art show to be something special for Smithville." A closed-lip smile brightened Mildred's face. "Audrey was right, you're a charmer." The smile left as fast as it appeared. "Your presence here tells me we're both early risers. Come to my home for coffee tomorrow morning at seven thirty."

The invitation sounded like a queen's edict, but he was glad to receive it. He'd spend time between students today thinking of questions to ask Mildred. If she was as cunning as he thought, she'd also be prepared tomorrow morning. What he really wanted to know was who had a reason for killing Lee Grimes. It seemed way too convenient that the knife used in the crime belonged to Mildred's nemesis, Riley Eastham.

Clayton stopped behind his mother, carrying two cardboard boxes of baked temptations. He nodded to Fen and asked, "How's the crown I put back on Thelma's tooth?"

"She has nothing but good things to say about it, and you."

Clayton flashed a toothy, white smile. "That's wonderful. Tell her to let me know if there's any pain at all."

Mildred had already closed the distance to the front door and stood waiting for her son to open it. "Come, Clayton. We've taken up enough of Sheriff Maguire's time."

Using his former title told Fen that Mildred knew much more about him than he did about her. Perhaps he could use his conversation with Bonnie Sterling to even the playing field. He'd need every advantage he could get tomorrow morning.

Chapter Twenty-One

Momentum in an investigation is a fickle thing. Fen sensed it moving, but knew it could easily grind to a halt or move in a direction that would take him even farther from the truth of who killed Lee Grimes.

What bothered him most was his inability to come up with a plausible motive. Lee wasn't a rich man, nor was he particularly smart. He didn't live in Smithville. Why did he come to the derelict piece of property by the river, owned by the city? Was he meeting someone? If so, why?

Could it be a drug deal gone bad? If that was true, a likely suspect might be Sonny Eastham. The police hadn't made that connection yet, even though the file reflected that they'd attempted to do so. Sonny's alibi was weak, stating he spent the night fishing. It was much more likely he passed out drunk, or was with a girl, or both.

What would Lou's trip to Dallas reveal? Even if she discovered Riley could have been in town when the murder took place, only his knife linked him to the crime scene. He could have lost it. Why had Audrey moved to Smithville two years prior? She fit into the community well and was in good graces with Mildred Fox. But why Smithville when she could be a big fish in a much bigger pond somewhere else?

He scratched the back of his head as he walked to the back door of Katy House. With all the stealth he could muster, he punched in the code and walked on tip-toes to the refrigerator. Two sack lunches sat inside. One for him and one with Ren's name on it.

A quick trip around the house brought him to Thelma's truck. Ren was climbing out of John's patrol car when he activated the key fob. She hollered, "You're running late."

Instead of hollering back, he watched John pull away before closing the distance between him and Ren. "Did you hear anything useful?"

Ren shook her head. "Cattle, grandchildren, and the weather were the major topics. Two women griped about how much traffic the art show would bring to town this weekend."

Fen pointed to the mural. "If you hope to finish by Friday night, you'd better do all you can today. Rain's coming."

"What will you do tomorrow?"

"I'm scheduling students to come here at assigned times. I'll see them in the living room."

Ren examined the mural. "I'll paint in my room if it rains. Bailey said she'll do the same."

A city patrol car drove by and Ren waved. "John's off duty now. There goes the first of his buddies. I'm counting to see how many times they check on me."

Fen asked, "Do you have your pepper spray?"

She pulled a small canister that looked like breath spray from her shirt pocket to show him.

"Good girl."

That ended the conversation, and he drove to the park overlooking the river. A minivan and a couple of other cars sat in the parking lot. Fen mounted the stairs to the observation deck where Bonnie stood in front of her easel. They traded good mornings as two anglers stood below them with fishing rods in hand.

Bonnie spent the next ten minutes explaining what she was trying to communicate in her painting. He was glad to see that she hadn't applied the first coat of background colors.

Fen took a long look. "It's a good idea, but sometimes less is more. Your log floating down the river is overpowering everything else. I like that you've shown the root ball, but the diameter of the log is much bigger than any of the other trees."

"I didn't want it to get lost and people miss the story."

"Trust the people viewing it and the story you're telling. Not everyone will understand what you're trying to communicate. In fact, most people won't. It's more important that they feel something than have words to tell you what it is they're feeling."

Fen then asked, "Why did you choose the river?"

Bonnie took her time responding. "It brings back wonderful memories, even though this is where Riley brought the body to shore.

"I used to work as a hospice nurse. Death ends one story and starts another. What I think about when I come here is all the people who have passed through my life. I also think of Riley rounding up teams of people to help clean the trash out of the river."

"Are environmental causes something he gets involved in regularly?"

Bonnie dusted eraser fibers from the canvas. "He's a good balance between new ideas and honoring the past. Trash in the river is a needless eyesore and a health hazard to people and wildlife. Before he came along and spearheaded the group you saw that day back in June, no one cleaned the river around Smithville." She paused. "That's only part of Riley's story."

"What's the rest?"

"I'm prejudiced because I'm in love with him, but Riley wants to see the town prosper. He's concerned about the deterioration of so many of the homes. There's a difference between reasonable historic preservation and watching homes go to rack and ruin."

She'd found her voice and showed no signs of slowing down without finishing her speech. "People gain self-worth by having good-paying jobs and decent homes to live in. The fastest way to accomplish that is to bring in new, high-paying jobs and build homes with modern, sustainable materials that don't rot or need painting every few years." She looked toward town. "Some people have remodeled with efficiency and the environment in mind, while so many other homes remain neglected. Those are better suited for termites than people."

She cast her gaze to him with an intensity that surprised him. "People read Riley wrong. He's a person who brings about change. Patience isn't his strong suit, but he wants to do good."

Fen pointed to her canvas. "Are you going to make the log smaller?"

"I'm changing it to a tree branch with a bird's nest in it. They're going to a new home."

He nodded. "That's a winner of a story. Since rain is forecast, come to the Katy House at nine o'clock in the morning and bring your canvas with background colors completed."

"I can see it all so clearly in my mind."

"Then paint it."

"I will."

"Good."

They both laughed. He got the idea that Bonnie wasn't one to climb on her soapbox to speak very often, but when she did, there was no holding her back. He wondered if her being so verbal would continue after he changed topics.

"I need to speak to you about something that happened after you left here yesterday. It involves your future stepson."

Her eyes opened wide and her voice filled with alarm. "What's he done now? Please tell me he didn't come on to Bailey."

The response told Fen the event wasn't Sonny's first experience with breaking the bounds of propriety. "Was he drinking?" asked Fen.

Bonnie dipped her head. "Drinking and drugs pretty much sum up his existence. He's been in and out of rehab facilities since he was fourteen, not to mention jail and prison." She brought her gaze back to Fen. "You're a former sheriff. Is Bailey going to file a police report on Sonny?"

"That's an option. Let me explain what he did. Then you can tell me what you think she should do."

Fen took his time and related the facts as Bailey reported them to him.

Bonnie heard him out and wagged her head. "Here we go again."

"What do you mean?"

"If there's one thing Sonny can do well, it's lie. I'm not trying to protect him anymore. He's very cunning so I don't expect he'll get in much trouble. He'll either deny everything or say Bailey encouraged him. Even if the cops can find the fisherman, Bailey didn't cry out for help."

Fen nodded. "That's why she didn't file a report."

A look of worry came into Bonnie's eyes. "What can we do for Sonny that we haven't already tried? Riley and I are at the end of our ropes." She corrected herself. "He may have an inch or two left on his, but I don't."

Fen puffed out his cheeks. "It's been my experience that

treatment works best when the person hits rock bottom and they make up their minds that they want to do the hard work that brings about change."

Bonnie's shoulders sagged. "You're not telling me anything I didn't already know. Still, you've helped me face reality. Sonny has to hit bottom."

Fen shifted his weight from one foot to the other. "I'm getting the impression that you're prepared for Sonny to suffer the consequences of his actions, but Riley isn't ready to cut him loose from support. What's it going to take for Riley to shift to your way of thinking?"

She spoke without thinking. "One good shove. He cut Sonny off from payments and insurance on his truck four months ago."

"Does he work enough to afford it?"

A weak laugh came from Bonnie. "Work is a four-letter word as far as Sonny is concerned."

"That tells me he's getting the money somewhere else. Any idea where?"

She shook her head. "I don't know, and frankly, I'm afraid to ask."

Fen was thinking about how to proceed when Bonnie spoke again. "You may think me a horrible person, but I'm more concerned about Riley than Sonny. Would you mind... I mean, could you talk to us together? You made a great impression on everyone when you took charge back in June. Riley and that young policeman didn't know what to do, but you guided them with authority. Then you backed off when experienced officers arrived."

"I don't have a crystal ball and can't see into the future. However, I do have years of experience dealing with people with problems like Sonny has. Bring Riley with you tomorrow."

Fen looked at his watch. He was running behind on allocating time with all his students. Inside, however, he was excited by the prospect of interviewing Riley without his attorney.

He rubbed his chin. "Nine in the morning may not be the best time. I have an early morning appointment tomorrow and the weatherman is sure it will rain. Why don't we move your appointment to the last of the day."

"That should work."

"Call and let me know if Riley can't or won't come."

"He'll come. He wants to know the status of the murder case."

"Why would he think I know anything?"

Bonnie issued a sly smile. "Come now, Sheriff Maguire. It's a small town. You and Audrey West were talking about something while you rocked on the front porch and you're meeting with Mildred Fox early tomorrow morning."

"Ah," he said. "The owner of the bakery has excellent hearing."

Bonnie let loose a guffaw. "It wasn't her. The old men who hang out there turn up their hearing aids."

"Serves me right for trying to eavesdrop on their conversations."

With plans made, Fen left the river and went to the lake southwest of town. Clouds were sparse and most of the artists were making adequate progress. The skill levels varied, but that came as no surprise. They all seemed to enjoy painting outside, except one redhead who failed to slather on sunblock. He examined her painting and told her to purchase a large tube of aloe vera on her way home. She'd done enough that she could finish her work indoors.

Fen ate a ham and cheese sandwich on his way to the state park. It was after three before he spoke to Bailey and Cory. Both seemed lost in their works. Cory was the first to break his concentration. "I may not know what I'm doing, but this is a lot more fun than I expected. Bailey told me I'd get in flow-state if I kept at it." He paused. "Or is it in a state of flow?"

Bailey huffed. "It's neither now that you've broken it."

Fen examined Cory's work. "Good lines. Try using bolder strokes, and more striking colors."

"That's what I've been telling him," said Bailey. "Maybe he'll listen to you. I might as well be talking to a tree stump."

"I know the feeling," said Fen. "There's a certain nineteen-year-old I know that has trouble taking advice."

Bailey growled.

Fen left, went to check on the remaining artists, and drove out of the park at fifteen before five. He wondered if Thelma had slept enough to carry her load as a night watchman.

Dark clouds scuttled across the sky, but something held back their moisture. Fen looked up through the top of the windshield. "Clouds holding moisture and people doing the same with information. Perhaps tomorrow both will break loose."

Chapter Twenty-Two

An explosion of light and sound shot through Fen's bedroom. A scream came from downstairs. His first response was to reach for his pistol on the nightstand. A thud sounded after he misjudged its distance and knocked the weapon to the floor. So much for protecting home, persons, and possessions.

He threw his feet off the bed and fought to make sense of what had happened. A second, more distant flash of light and a roll of thunder revealed the truth of what had interrupted his dreamless slumber. Lightning had struck hard nearby. He moved to the windows streaked by wind-driven sheets of water. The covered porch downstairs would give him a better view. Thelma had screamed, and he needed to check on her.

The rattled woman met him at the bottom of the stairs. "Lord, have mercy! If that lightning was any closer, it would have been under the blanket with me." She paused. "Do you smell something?"

Fen nodded. "I'll look outside. You go upstairs and check all the bedrooms. If you see or smell smoke, come down as quickly as you can. The attic may be on fire."

Fen spun the lock on the door and exited to the porch. Driving rain hit his legs and bare feet with drops that felt like ice cubes. He looked to his left and moved closer to the edge of the porch. Puffs of smoke and a hissing sound came from one of the massive pecan trees. An ominous creaking sound intensified as a gust of wind seemed intent on continuing the pre-dawn destruction. One more mighty gust separated the tree, with half of it tumbling earthward.

Fen held his breath and hoped for the best. He moved into the front yard to get a better view. Not believing his eyes, he moved to the edge of the home. The tree hadn't split in half but at a Y in the two main branches. One remained attached to the trunk while the second lay between the Katy House and the home next door. The large lot had saved both homes from extensive damage.

There wasn't a dry thread on him when he went back into the house. Thelma met him. "Are we going to live?"

"I can almost guarantee we'll see daylight."

"In that case, don't move. You're dripping like a wet dog. I'll run upstairs and get you a couple of towels."

Bailey's voice sounded from the direction of the dining room. "Who fired the cannon?"

"I'm at the front door," hollered Fen.

She came into view with strands of wet, blond hair framing her face. A fleece throw covered her scanty sleepwear. Ren followed. She'd maintained modesty by arriving in Wonder Woman pajamas with a towel over her head.

Cory staggered in last, dressed much like Fen, wearing jeans, a wet T-shirt, and barefoot. Both men still held their pistols. Fen cleared his throat. "We can put these away for now. I don't think the tree outside will give us any more trouble."

Thelma spoke from the top of the stairs. "It's almost five. I'll have coffee ready in ten minutes, or you can go back to bed."

She continued her downward trek. "Fen, you get in a hot shower. I can hear your teeth chattering from here." She threw a towel at him. "Dry off with this and I'll wipe up the mess you made."

Fen didn't argue.

A knock on the door sounded before Fen could take a step. He opened it and John entered. "Is everyone all right? That tree out front is still smoldering."

Ren became the group's spokesperson. "We're fine. Talk about starting the day with a bang."

John looked at her and wagged his head. "Do you always sleep in that?"

"Of course not; that would be boring. I like to mix things up, mostly with Marvel comic characters. Have you ever been to a comic con?"

"Can't say that I have." He turned to Fen. "I need to go. The storm is causing damage everywhere, and it's not over yet. You're lucky you still have power."

John's quick departure showed Fen that the young patrolman was serious about his job. He closed the door, shutting out the chilly wind that had filled the foyer.

The artist in Fen came to the surface as he considered the contrast between the formality of John's uniform and Ren's choice of sleepwear. It confirmed his belief that their relationship would be shallow and brief.

Fen followed Thelma's instructions to warm himself in a hot shower. His thoughts turned to the morning's appointment with Mildred Fox.

By the time he had a cup of coffee and unlocked his truck, the driving deluge had morphed into a steady rain. As with all journeys in Smithville, the drive to Mildred's home didn't take long. He parked by the curb and examined the structure. It surprised him that the Greek Revival home wasn't the most striking in town. Like the *Hope Floats* house, the front boasted covered porches on both the ground level and the second story, but the differences were striking.

The half-moon porches of the home made popular by a movie softened it visually, giving it a warm, welcoming, peaceful feel. Not so with what he dubbed The Fox House. Right angles and perfect symmetry were this home's hallmarks. It also lacked the massive trees and a view of the river. He theorized the patriarch of the Fox clan chose the property for its proximity to commerce, as it stood on a rather barren corner lot within two blocks of the main road through town. Perhaps lightning had struck a majestic shade-maker several decades ago leaving it treeless.

Fen looked forward to seeing the inside of the home. Mildred Fox didn't impress him as a woman who'd skimp on quality. He followed a pristine sidewalk to the five steps leading up to the front porch, which was void of chairs or a porch swing. He thought it a waste of a perfectly good place to rock and wave at neighbors. Two massive planters guarded the front door, which was painted black to match the shutters on each side of every window.

The ringing of the doorbell didn't bring an immediate response. Fen was looking out to the street when locks turned and the door behind him opened. He spun and beheld a woman wearing the all-black uniform of a housekeeper. "Mr. Maguire?"

He nodded.

"Please, come in. Mrs. Fox is expecting you."

The woman walked with a limp. Fen attributed it to the gout that Mildred had mentioned the day before.

It was a slow walk through the spotless foyer. The odor of

lemon oil polish rose from the antique furniture. A framed portrait caught his eye and stopped his forward progress. The woman in the painting was not only lovely, but the artist had done an exceptional job of capturing her. The expression on the blond beauty's face was a fascinating mix of wedding jitters and excitement.

Fen moved closer and examined the bride's blue eyes. It surprised him when he read sadness buried deep in them.

The maid had backtracked. "That's Dr. Fox's late wife. She was a dentist like him, but she died a long time ago. He never remarried."

All Fen could do was swallow hard and move on. He found himself in a room with a collection of baroque chairs and a couch, each sitting perpendicular to the fireplace. The paintings on the walls looked as if someone had measured the gaps between them with a micrometer.

Fen waited for Mildred to speak first. "You arrived precisely on time, Mr. Maguire. Please, have a seat on the couch."

He did as instructed. "That was quite a storm. Did you receive any damage?"

"Not to my knowledge, but I understand there's minor flooding in the usual places."

It seemed Mildred wasn't overly concerned with the weather, so he remained silent. She instructed her housekeeper to pour coffee and make sure Fen had his choice of treats from a silver tray. He saw that balancing a cup and plate on his lap would be a challenge, so he told her he'd already eaten. The maid hobbled out of the room, leaving them alone.

"I'd like to know what progress you've made in solving the murder of that ne'er-do-well from Bastrop. And please don't pretend to be surprised that I know you're in town helping the police."

Fen hesitated, not because he didn't expect the question, but because he wanted to see how she'd react when he delayed.

"Please, Sheriff, speak freely."

He hiked his right boot over his left knee. "The local police responded to the murder with speed and made excellent decisions. The first and best was to call for a task force to investigate. That brought in personnel and resources from the county, state, and even federal levels. Their investigation was thorough and resulted in a quick arrest."

"You're omitting one major thing. They arrested the wrong man."

Fen held up a hand. "I'm not yet willing to go along with that conclusion."

Her eyes opened wide, revealing something he hadn't noticed before. Her drooping eyelids hooded two emerald irises. She all but barked out, "Do you have proof?"

"Not yet."

Her eyes narrowed. "Oh. That's too bad."

Fen moved on with haste. "So far, it's only a hunch based on experience." He brought his boot to the floor. "If further investigation shows that Riley has a bulletproof alibi, he'll go free. The only physical evidence the police have is his knife, which I believe he will claim to have lost weeks earlier."

"That could be a lie."

"The possibility of a defendant lying to protect himself is true in every criminal or civil case. The odds of others lying for him go down. Serving time for perjury is something most people won't chance. A skilled investigator can spot it and deal with it."

"Someone like you?"

Fen responded with a grin. "I used to be pretty good. I'm mainly an artist now." He didn't give her a chance to respond. "What's your impression of Riley Eastham?"

"He belongs in a big city."

"I haven't spoken to him yet, but that's the impression I'm getting. From what I understand, he'd like to see big changes made to the town."

Mildred shifted in her chair. "You may not believe this, Mr. Maguire, but I'm a proponent of change as long as it's deliberative and doesn't tear the fabric of the town to shreds."

Fen scratched his head. "That sounds reasonable, but so does the desire to attract new industries, businesses, jobs, and housing."

"You sound like a campaign spokesman for Mr. Eastham."

He held up two hands. "Don't shoot the messenger. I'm repeating what I hear."

"Perhaps you're talking to the wrong people."

"That's why I'm here."

A voice sounded from the direction of the hallway that Fen assumed led to the stairway. He leaned forward to rise. Clayton Fox arrived wearing dark blue medical garb with his name and title embroidered over his heart.

"Good morning, Mr. Maguire." He shifted his gaze. "Hello, Mother. I see you survived the storm."

Her only response was, "There's coffee on the sideboard, along with something for your sweet tooth. Mr. Maguire and I were discussing the intricacies of a murder investigation. He believes there's a chance Riley Eastham's alibi isn't as air-tight as the police think it is."

Fen said, "It's not just the police, but the district attorney, too." He flipped his hand in a sign of dismissal. "It's only a theory at this point."

The dentist took a seat in the chair next to his mother. "Have you considered Sonny Eastham? After getting to know Riley on the city council, I'd say his son is more likely to get carried away and hurt someone."

"I'm taking a fresh look at everyone, but it's going to take time. Having to meet with artists all day this week is a bit of a hindrance. Basically, I'm spending most of my free time reviewing what's already in the police file."

"Have you found anything amiss?" asked Mildred.

"That's the interesting thing." Fen allowed a few ticks of the clock to pass so tension could build. "No one has a decent motive for killing Lee Grimes."

"Does there have to be one?" asked Clayton.

"Not always, but I'm willing to place a small wager that someone had an excellent reason to murder Lee Grimes. I just haven't figured out what that reason is." He lowered his voice. "Not yet."

"Do you think you will?" asked Clayton.

Fen stood. "Every year there are thousands of homicides that go unsolved. I've been lucky so far. Perhaps it's time for me to strike out in the bottom of the ninth and lose the game."

Mildred cast a cool gaze toward the fireplace that didn't appear to have ever provided warmth. "I'm disappointed in your lack of progress, Mr. Maguire."

"Things can change suddenly in murder investigations." He stood. "I'll show myself out."

Fen made his way down the front steps. So much for keeping his role in the investigation under wraps. It amazed him how hard it was to keep a secret in a small town. And to top it off, the interview hadn't revealed the results he'd hoped for.

He was halfway to his truck when he received a text from Audrey.

Sonny Eastham shot. Ambulance on scene.

Chapter Twenty-Three

The text message said a lot, but not nearly enough. Fen took long strides toward his truck as he re-read the brief text. It hadn't changed. Sonny Eastham was on his way to receive treatment for a gunshot wound.

The words *how, who,* and *where* buzzed in Fen's brain like flies at a summer picnic. He thrust his right hand into the pocket of his jeans to retrieve his keys. The wail of a siren caused his head to jerk around. The mechanical screams sounded from the direction of the river. Looking, he saw nothing. The sound decreased. This told him the emergency vehicle had turned. Could it be the ambulance carrying Sonny Eastham to the local hospital? Perhaps it was another first responder arriving at the scene?

He longed to fire up his truck and follow the siren's wails, but he wasn't a first responder and he'd only be in the way. His place was back at Katy House, waiting for information to come to him and helping artists improve their paintings. Still, he needed to do something, so he called Bailey.

"Have you and Cory left yet?"

"You're using your cop voice. What's going on?"

"Is Ren with you?"

"Yeah. We're all fine. We heard all kinds of sirens and thought it had something to do with flooding from the storm."

"I received a report that Sonny Eastham's hurt."

"Hurt? How?"

"Shot. I don't have any details."

"Holy moly. What can we do?"

"Nothing. Stay inside and paint. This is one of those times when we have to be patient."

"We can't paint in the main house."

"Why not?"

"Thelma's sleeping on the couch."

Fen hadn't realized his wipers were making intermittent swipes across his windshield. "Oh. I'm on my way. She can be grumpy if you try to get her to move."

"Duh! Do you need to get some coffee in you to get your brain working?"

"It's working fine."

Bailey then asked, "Who told you about Sonny? I bet it was Mildred Fox. She knows everything going on in Smithville."

"It was Audrey."

"She must have you on speed dial."

Fen ignored the implication behind Bailey's statement. "Let's try to be extra quiet today. Thelma needs to sleep."

"If she sleeps all day, she'll be up all night."

Fen huffed. "That's the idea."

He imagined Bailey shaking her head as she said, "I don't get it. Sonny's been shot. He's either dead, dying, or in the hospital. And you're worried about waking up Thelma instead of going to the crime scene?"

"I'll go when it's time. I'm almost to the B&B."

Calling the owner of the Katy House and reporting the lightning strike hadn't occurred to him until he pulled to the curb. Two cars pulled up behind him. A woman in her forties with broad shoulders and narrow hips exited the car and began snapping photos. She approached him.

"Sir," she began. "I'm a reporter for the local newspaper. Are you staying here?"

Fen groaned. He hadn't thought of Lou being out of town and missing out on this story, or the much bigger scoop of Sonny being shot. He hated to lie to the reporter, but he wasn't in the mood to explain who he was or why he was in town. Perhaps he could give the reporter a dab of truth and get her to move on.

"I'm from out of town, and was driving by when I saw this." He pointed to the downed portion of the tree. "It looks like lightning struck and cut it in half. The people who own this house are lucky. It missed their home and the one next door."

The woman put a hint of pride in her voice. "This is The Katy House. It's rated as one of the top bed-and-breakfasts in the state."

"You don't say."

"It's a fact. People from all over include The Katy House on their vacation schedules."

He looked down the street as two more vehicles parked behind the reporter. "News of the tree being struck by lightning must be getting around. I'd better make room for sightseers."

Fen didn't slow down until he was in the cab of his truck. He brought it to life, pulled around the corner, and parked in front of the next house. The novelty of such a massive tree almost damaging the historic home and business would hold the reporter and sightseers for a while.

A thought came to him. Perhaps he had time to get back in Lou's good graces. Where should he look first? The hospital? No. First, he'd make sure things were going okay inside the house.

Fen backtracked down the street and entered through the kitchen door. Instead of sleeping, Thelma was washing dishes. "I hope you're not hungry. The kitchen's closed."

"Bailey said you were sleeping."

"Well, I'm not now," she snapped.

He changed the subject. "Here's a bit of news that will affect you. I don't know the details yet, but Sonny Eastham got himself shot. He should be at the hospital by now. That means you don't have to stay awake tonight."

Thelma narrowed her eyes. "Is that all the details you're going to tell me?"

"It's all I know."

She let out a huff. "How did you ever solve a case?" She threw down her dishtowel. "I'll be in my room and I'm not coming out until I know what's going on in this town."

He considered asking her to let him know what she found out but realized she was in no mood.

Bailey, Cory, and Ren breezed into the kitchen in time to hear Thelma's bedroom door slam shut. Bailey gave him her tilted-head-and-raised-eyebrows look. It was her way of asking, *What's wrong with Thelma?*

"Tired, and I don't have details on the shooting yet." Fen continued. "She's probably a little homesick, too."

Bailey corrected him. "If she's homesick, it's for her network of spies."

Fen didn't correct her.

His phone buzzed in the pocket of his shirt. He plucked it out and looked at the name on the screen.

"Hey, Lou. How's Big D?"

"Too big. I understand the county got hit hard last night."

"Early this morning," said Fen. "Lightning hit one of the big trees by the street out front. Split it almost in two. Half the tree is lying in the yard by the side of the house. Curious locals are lining up to see it."

"Did it hurt anyone or cause damage?"

"Only to the tree."

Lou became philosophical. "The threshold for what makes a newsworthy story lowers in proportion to the number of miles an event is from a major metropolitan area. That may be big news in Smithville, but nowhere else."

"That's only one story," said Fen. "I wish you were here. You're missing something bigger than a charred tree in the yard. Audrey sent me a brief text this morning. I'll pull it up and read it to you." He did so and waited for a response.

"Have you called Audrey back?"

"Not yet."

Lou's words became more clipped. "What about all your contacts in law enforcement?"

"No, and Thelma's not pleased that I don't know more."

"She can join the sisterhood of the under-informed. First, you send me to Dallas on a fool's errand. So far, Riley Eastham's alibis check out. Next, in a town where nothing much ever happens, you have major storm damage and a shooting. Not to mention that the shooting involves a suspect in a murder investigation."

She rang off and Fen dropped his phone in a pocket. Like the storm effect on the town, Lou seemed soaked in disappointment. Fen knew that her emotional storms usually passed quickly; all he had to do was provide her details of the shooting.

He piled into his truck, cranked the already warm engine, and wasted no time in leaving the scene where nature had assaulted the towering tree and likely killed it. As he pulled onto the street, an interesting thought occurred to him. He was leaving nature's crime scene to find another caused by a human.

Chapter Twenty-Four

F en believed in intuition... about seventy-five percent of the time. On this occasion, it was telling him where to go. He knew he was on the right track when a sheriff's department SUV passed him running hot with lights and siren. The vehicle led him straight to what looked like an impromptu gathering of first responders near the *Hope Floats* house.

Fen parked at the nearest open spot, which was a block away from the rutted gravel road leading to the river bottom. He anchored his straw cowboy hat on his head, walked fast, and tried to look worried. It wasn't a foolproof method of getting close to a crime scene, but it worked on this occasion. The heavy drizzle of rain also helped, as he wasn't the only person wearing a rain jacket.

Luck was on his side when he saw Ben Crump's truck parked on the floodplain. Ben was in the cab, talking on his phone.

Fen knocked on the passenger side window, and Ben motioned for him to enter. The phone call ended by the time Fen settled into the seat.

Ben spoke without prompting. "A single gunshot to the chest, away from the heart. EMTs said he's lucky. He's young and strong and there was no indication it went through his lung. They'll stabilize him here at the local hospital. If needed, they'll fly him to a trauma center in Austin."

"Was he conscious?"

Ben nodded. "Conscious, scared, and not talking about what happened. He was more interested in talking to a lawyer than a doctor."

Fen took in the information and said, "That's interesting." He scanned the scene and noted the police tape that formed a large rectangle. "Anything unusual about the crime scene?"

"Yeah. No footprints, except those of the first responders. Sonny was wearing boots that had no mud on them."

Fen nodded. "That means the shooting took place before the rain started. It also means that the rain washed away all traces of whoever shot him."

"Yep, and there's more. Sonny called it in himself, but not until long after the worst of the storm blew through."

Fen jerked his head to the left. "He must have been unconscious."

"That's what everyone is saying."

Fen changed the subject. "It's quite a coincidence that this shooting took place where someone killed Lee Grimes."

"Yep," said Ben, again. "It comes as no surprise that someone shot Sonny, but why here?" Ben continued, "The locals are talking about it being a drug deal gone bad."

"Any evidence of that?"

"Nope."

Fen huffed. "I can tell you're getting close to retirement. You're using 'yep' and 'nope' more often."

Ben looked out the window. "Good luck solving this one without me. I was told last night I'm going on a cruise. My wife found one with belly-dancing classes. I told her to count me out of anything but watching."

Fen didn't stuff down the explosion of laughter. "No wonder you're distracted." He reached for the door handle. "Thanks for the information and enjoy the cruise."

"Yep."

Fen didn't wait to arrive at his truck to call Lou. He pressed his phone against his ear and avoided eye contact with everyone as he walked up the muddy path.

"I'm still mad at you," said Lou.

"I'm leaving the crime scene. A local newspaper reporter is at the Katy House doing a story on lightning striking one of the pecan trees out front."

Fen could sense Lou bristling with anticipation. "Are there any other reporters covering the shooting?"

"Not yet. Do you have a pen and paper?"

"You're so old school. I'll record our conversation."

Lou waited until he'd finished telling her everything he'd heard, except for Ben's upcoming cruise.

"Who's your source?" asked Lou.

"You can't use his name, but it's Ben Crump."

"I can live with that. He's reliable." She then asked, "What do you make of the location being the same as the murder?"

"It's suspicious."

"Is there a possibility the gunshot was self-inflicted?"

"Ben would have mentioned it. The locals think it's related to drugs."

"That's what they default to when they don't know. What do you think?"

Fen approached his truck and pulled out his keys. "I need to get back to the house and you have a story to write. When are you coming back to Smithville?"

"I have one more lead to follow up on, then write and sell

this story. I'll be back tonight. There's more going on in Smithville than there is in Dallas."

"I bet that's the first time anyone ever said that."

Lou had one more question. "Am I free to speculate?"

"Let your imagination run, but not too far. Base everything on facts and turn up the heat. There's something rotten in this small town and someone's kept it on ice too long."

The call ended without a salutation. Typical for Lou when she had a story to write. He knew that she'd scoop the local reporter and Mildred Fox would throw a fit. So be it. Murder was an ugly business.

It wasn't long before Fen arrived back at the B&B. He parked on 2nd Street, away from the crowd who came to gawk at the tree. He entered through the back door and found Thelma puttering in the kitchen.

She explained without his prompting. "Still too much going on this morning to sleep. Bailey, Ren, and Cory want to paint in the dining room. If they spill anything on the floor, carpets, or furniture, they'll clean it themselves."

"I can tell them to paint in their rooms."

She didn't say anything, but Thelma's posture told him she believed the trio would prefer to band together in the house. She could be right. If so, they'd need to rearrange the furniture in the dining room.

Fen changed the subject. "Sonny received one gunshot to the right side of his chest. He's at the local hospital."

Bailey pushed open the swinging door to the kitchen. "Serves him right."

Fen ignored her comment and asked, "Where do you want to paint?"

"We'd like to stay together, but don't want to interfere with your students."

Fen pointed to the dining room. "Let's move the table and

chairs to one side of the room. Put down drop cloths and be careful. Whatever you do, don't block the kitchen door. Thelma might want to take a nap at some point."

Bailey turned to Ren and Cory. "You heard him. It's a full day of painting."

The doorbell's ring was Fen's signal to welcome his first student of the day. It surprised him to see Bonnie Sterling when he opened the door. She stepped into the foyer and blurted out, "Riley isn't coming, and I may have to leave at any time. Someone shot Sonny."

Fen expressed what he hoped would be the correct blend of shock and sympathy. "That's terrible. Don't you need to go to the hospital?"

"Riley says there's no reason for both of us to be there. The injury isn't life-threatening, but they're admitting him for observation. Riley said the police may arrest him. If they do, it won't be the first time he's gone from a hospital to a jail cell."

"He's not under arrest?"

"The police are telling him he will be if he doesn't tell them who shot him. Riley says it's a bogus charge of obstructing a police investigation, but it may be enough to revoke his parole." She took in a long breath and let it out slowly. "It may be best if he goes back to prison."

"Are you and Riley in agreement on that?"

Bonnie gave her head a single nod. "Riley told the cops he's not spending any more money on attorneys." After dabbing her eyes with a tissue, she brought her gaze back to Fen. "Sonny cooked his goose when he wouldn't tell Riley where he got the money for a huge down payment on that new truck."

"How much did that set him back?"

"Ten grand—and he's made at least four payments of over eight hundred dollars since then. Add to that monthly insurance and gasoline. It has to cost him well over a thousand dollars a month to ride around in that fancy truck. That's hard to do when you're not working."

Fen took in the information but changed the subject. "Is your painting in the car?"

She tapped her forehead with her palm. "I'm such a dunce. I should have brought it in."

Every fiber of Fen's being wanted to go upstairs and paint until his mind was completely clear. Once that happened, he believed the scraps of information would fall into place. Perhaps that was only a pleasant daydream, but he didn't think so. Answers often came when he hit the flow state of painting. Unfortunately, that wasn't in the cards for today. Bonnie soon returned with her painting, then his next artist arrived early.

The morning proved to be one artist arriving after another, all eager to receive tips and pointers that would make their works attract attention at the weekend's show and sale.

Fen had scheduled a thirty-minute break for lunch, but even that didn't work out. He watched through the living room window as the morning's last student skipped down the steps with canvas in hand and walked to his car. As he pulled away, Audrey pulled into the vacated spot.

Chapter Twenty-Five

F en stepped onto the front porch as Audrey got out of her car. The rain had stopped, and the slate-gray sky was breaking apart. He checked the condition of the rocking chairs. To his surprise, they felt dry.

The heels of Audrey's shoes clicked their way along the sidewalk and up the wooden steps. She wore a business suit that fit snug in all the right places and showed off her assets in a demure, yet alluring sort of way. The muted colors made her emerald eyes shine even brighter than he remembered. Her mane of black hair was gathered at the back, giving her facial features a chance to show off.

Fen swallowed and lifted his chin. "Good afternoon, counselor. Has your day been as busy as mine?"

She flashed a coy smile. "If it was half as busy as mine, I'd say we both need some time off this evening."

He sensed an invitation coming but waited a tick too long to head it off.

"There's a hamlet north of town called Winchester. Believe it or not, they have some of the best steaks you can find in the entire state. You look like a man who could use a medium-rare ribeye. Or are you a T-bone sort of cowboy?"

"Both, but only one per night."

She tilted her head. "No, I think you could handle two if you put your mind to it."

He cleared his throat and changed the subject as quickly as he could. "I went to the crime scene and spoke with Ben. He told me the basics, then called me back with more details. It seems someone was a lousy shot."

Audrey huffed as she sat down. "I thought you'd be ready to talk about something besides crime. Oh well, if we have to, let's discuss Sonny Eastham. The responding officers said there were powder burns on his shirt."

"Someone was up close and personal."

Audrey shook her head. "It was a through-and-through. The doc said the lung had to be deflated or the bullet would have clipped it. That's a lucky break to miss a rib and the lung."

Fen could almost see the wound. "What's your theory?"

"The same as yours. It was a warning to Sonny. A very serious warning. He's in over his head with someone."

"That makes sense. It also makes sense that the cops would be wondering how he affords that truck he drives without a job."

"Drugs, I guess."

"That's one possibility," said Fen.

"What's another?"

Fen hooked a boot over a knee. "I'll let you know when I think of it."

Audrey cut her eyes to look at him. "Why do I sense you've already thought of four or five other possibilities?"

"Artists have active imaginations. We see many things that aren't there."

"Can you see us going for a beer tonight? It's only two blocks away."

"First, it's a thick steak. And now, a beer with a beautiful woman. I'd be a fool to turn down offers like those." He paused. "But..." He allowed the word to trail off.

Audrey put her hand over her heart. "Here it comes—the big rejection. I can feel my heart breaking."

"Lou's coming back from Dallas this evening. She's bringing information that will show if Riley could have been in town when his knife killed Lee Grimes."

"That's not a good enough excuse for making me cry, but I'll accept it this time. Perhaps when this is all over, we can go to Winchester and have a steak."

Fen spoke before thinking. "That would be a nice way to celebrate solving the murder and the assault." He then asked, "How much heat is the chief of police catching for another serious crime on city property?"

Audrey stood. "Mildred is sharpening her knives. If you don't solve these crimes by the next city council meeting, I'd say the chief needs to rent a U-Haul."

Fen slid his boot from his knee and stood. "At least there's no pressure."

"A big, strong lawman like you should be able to handle Mildred."

"Former lawman, and I lift paintbrushes instead of weights."

"That reminds me. Do you paint portraits?"

"Not anymore. Only landscapes, and caricatures if I'm giving Bailey a break at a fair of some sort."

"That's a shame. I always wanted a portrait of me and John. You know, the mother-son sort of thing."

"Bailey could do it. Or, I could refer you to other competent artists who specialize in portraits."

She lifted her chin. "I think I know why you don't paint portraits, but I'll not tell you."

"That's good," said Fen. "I wouldn't tell you if you're right or wrong."

She walked toward the steps and turned. "I won't bother you again until you solve the murder and the assault." Her emerald eyes flashed with mischief. "Then it's off to Winchester. I'll order a rib eye and you'll get a T-bone. We'll trade bites until we're both satisfied."

It felt like a rock lodged in his throat. He'd never met a woman who could make eating steak sound so intriguing.

He was watching her walk down the sidewalk when Bailey came through the door. He cleared his throat and tried to clear his brain.

Bailey looked at Audrey as the attorney walked like a cat to her car. After the door shut, she commented. "That's a nice swing she has in her backyard."

"I hadn't noticed," said Fen.

Bailey let out a guffaw. "All men notice." The mirth left her voice. "Why is she coming on so strong to you?"

Fen had no comment on the remark other than, "Is there anything to eat?"

"There's always something when Thelma is in the house. What do you want?"

"Anything but steak."

"Huh?"

"Never mind. I'll find something. My next student will arrive soon."

Fen spent the afternoon coaching students of varying levels of skill and ambition. The vibration of Bailey's question seemed to hang in the air, and he couldn't help but replay it in his mind. Why was Audrey coming on so strong?

He couldn't deny she had forced her way into his thoughts.

Audrey seemed to know how to stir him in ways that he'd reserved only for his late wife, Sally. But why? Did she really want a relationship with him, or was there an ulterior motive? If so, his imagination didn't stretch far enough to know what it could be. Her son was the center of her universe.

Questions without answers continued to come and go as the afternoon progressed. Why had Audrey called him earlier that day to report the shooting? Why did she flirt so blatantly? Did she see him as a candidate to grow old with? He wasn't over the hill yet, but mirrors weren't as friendly as they once were.

He added another question to his list. Was Audrey connected to either the murder or the shooting? He hoped not, but that wouldn't stop him from digging into her past or reexamining the thick file Chuck and Candy had compiled for him.

Two hours into his afternoon appointments his phone rang. He excused himself from the presence of an artist with a genuine gift for gab, but not for painting. On the way to the front door, he addressed the caller. "Hold on, Candy. Let me go out on the porch."

"Am I interrupting something important?" asked Lawyer Chuck's wife.

"You're giving my ears a much-needed break. Did you find out anything interesting about Audrey West or her son?"

"Yes, and no. There's a steel political curtain around Audrey and a double curtain protecting John. I was told to back off. The attorney who spoke with Chuck wasn't so polite."

Fen was silent for several seconds. "That tells me Audrey told the truth about John's father."

"Do you think there's any chance she's involved in the case you're working on?"

"It's cases now. Someone shot one of my suspects this morning."

"We heard. What's the latest medical report?"

"No serious damage. He's either the luckiest man I've ever met or something really fishy is going on. You probably already know that the police are considering arresting him in hopes the parole board will send him back to prison. I've sent word to the chief to give me a few more days before he takes any action."

Candy reverted to her reason for calling. "Is delving into Audrey's past essential for solving the case?"

"If you're asking if I have to know who John's biological father is, the answer is no. That doesn't mean I won't look farther back into Audrey's past or dig deeper into why she's living in Smithville. There are a few things niggling at my mind, but they look like shadows on a foggy night."

"If it has anything to do with John's father, leave them in the fog. It would also be best if you could keep Audrey's name away from the press."

"That might not be possible."

"You might be Superman, but her son is kryptonite. Proceed at your own risk."

"Thanks, Candy. Tell Chuck I said hello."

"He doesn't want to hear from you until everything's quietly wrapped up. Hopefully, that's soon and certain secrets remain undisturbed."

Fen didn't respond to the poorly veiled meaning behind Candy's words. Do enough to solve the obvious crimes, but leave certain things buried. The problem with any investigation is that the truth doesn't like to be buried. Light has a way of poking itself into the dark corners of people's lives.

As he walked into the house, his thoughts strayed to Lou and whether her time in Dallas would shine a light on what Riley Eastham might be hiding. He didn't believe it would, but, then again...

Chapter Twenty-Six

F en was looking out the living room window when Lou pulled her Camry next to the curb. Long shadows from a tired sun matched Fen's mood. The day had started early, been filled to the brim with work, and now he needed to rest. Unfortunately, he knew that wasn't to be, as Lou breezed in and dropped her travel bag at the bottom of the stairs. Bailey, Cory, and Ren had moved their paintings and supplies back to their rooms and were taking a break before supper. They might have told him their plans for the evening, but he didn't think so. Either way, he'd reached a saturation point for new information. Or, at least, he thought he had. Lou's words changed his mind.

"It took much longer than I thought, but I have conclusive evidence that Riley Eastham wasn't in Dallas on at least one day that he claimed he was." She gave the exact day as Fen digested one more bite of information.

Instead of interrupting her, Fen waited for an explanation.

Lou lifted her chin in self-adulation. "He drove to Bastrop for a business luncheon, then drove back to Dallas."

"A business luncheon?"

"With an attorney and a housing developer." She moved toward the couch and sat down. "There was one more man there, but the young woman at the restaurant didn't recognize him. She remembered they each left a cash tip."

"Did she catch anything they said?"

Lou responded with a shake of her head. "It was a busy day, and she had other tables to take care of."

Fen sat in one of the chairs in front of the window he'd been looking out of. He took in the information and processed it. He needed more facts. "Other than the one day in Bastrop, were you able to verify Riley was in Dallas all the other days?"

Lou nodded. "Everything else lines up with what's in the file. I guess the cops missed Riley going out the back door of the hotel. I'm sure they were watching for his truck to leave the parking lot, but he drove Bonnie's car to Dallas that day."

Fen puffed out his cheeks. "When did he return to the hotel in Dallas?"

"Early evening; he came through the front door at six-thirty."

"That makes it technically possible for him to kill Lee Grimes, but unlikely. He'd have to drive from Bastrop to Smithville immediately after leaving the restaurant, have Lee meet him at the vacant lot, kill him in broad daylight, then hurry back to Dallas. That's too many steps, and too risky. Everyone in town knows him."

Lou posed the best question of the day. "Then why did he risk a perjury charge by giving the police a false statement?"

Fen had no answer, but he was determined to find out. "I want you to go to Bastrop tomorrow. See if you can find additional details of Riley's meeting. Talk to the attorney and the housing developer. Do all you can to discover the identity of the mystery man."

"What will you do?"

"I'll ask Riley why he lied to the police."

"I'd like to be there when you ask."

Fen shook his head. "You might scare him into not talking. Besides, you'll be busy in Bastrop. I'll tell you everything that happens."

She stuck out her bottom lip in protest, but didn't press the issue other than to say, "I guess I owe you that much for calling me back with the story of the shooting this morning." Her eyebrows raised. "Any other stories you're keeping from me?"

"Would you believe me if I said no?"

"Ha. You tell no one but Sally all you know."

"That's because she's the only person I ever fully trusted."

Lou cleared her throat. "You must have had a pocket full of four-leaf clovers when you tricked Sally into marrying you. I'm thinking that finding someone I can trust is a lost cause." She smiled. "Except for present company."

An image of Audrey flashed in Fen's mind. The green-eyed beauty didn't qualify as someone he could trust, but he didn't know why. His lower jaw came down in a yawn. "My blood sugar must be low. Let's see what Thelma has for us to eat tonight. I bet you're starving after that long drive from Dallas."

"I snacked on spicy potato chips until my lips and mouth were on fire. What's left of the half-eaten bag is on the back floorboard of my car. I threw it where I couldn't reach it." She heaved a sigh. "Crummy men and awful food are my downfall."

Fen lifted a hand and pointed toward the dining room. "Thelma can help you with the food, but I wouldn't mention anything about crummy men. She's been gathering information all week. There's no telling what hair-raising stories she could tell."

"Don't worry about that," said Lou. "It's supper, then bed

for me." She looked at him. "What about you? You look worn around the edges."

"I don't doubt it, but there's a thick file that I need to re-read."

Lou sat up straighter. "That usually means you're getting close to solving the case."

Bailey's voice rang out as she hit the bottom stair. "Is that true? Are you close?"

Fen held up his hand. "Hold on, you two. I never said that."

"You don't have to," said Bailey. "There's nothing in that file that you don't already know. If you're going over it again, it means you're putting the pieces together."

Lou nodded with vigor. "I learned today that Riley Eastham lied to the police."

Bailey's eyes widened. "I don't trust him."

Fen let out a huff. "You've never met Riley."

"That may be, but I met his son, and they say an acorn doesn't fall far from its tree."

Thelma walked in from the dining room and joined the chorus. "That's right. I heard an earful today about all the things Sonny Eastham's done in his brief life. That boy is trouble with a capital T. If only half of them are true, they need to lock him up and weld the door to his cell shut. His daddy can't be much better."

Fen countered with, "It's my understanding about half the town says Riley is an upstanding citizen."

Thelma nodded. "And the other half don't trust him."

"Riley has no criminal record," said Fen.

"Not yet," said Lou.

"It's only a matter of time," said Thelma. "It was his knife that killed that man from Bastrop."

Bailey asked, "Didn't he say he lost it? That's a convenient excuse."

Fen held up both hands as stop signs. "Stop and listen to yourselves. Whenever a suspect gives you a plausible explanation, it's the duty of the investigator to either prove it or disprove it. Speculation won't cut it."

Lou dipped her head. "Fen's right."

Thelma tented her hands on her hips. "The police should have asked him where he lost it."

Bailey shook her head. "They did, and he said he didn't know. His lawyer told him to say nothing else about the knife."

Fen showed he agreed by saying, "It's the job of the police to find out where he lost the knife."

Thelma scoffed and said, "Then they need to get busy doing their job."

Fen closed his eyes and lowered his voice. "They tried, but where do you look if the suspect won't talk to you?"

No one answered until Fen broke the silence. "That's it."

"What's it?" asked Lou.

"He won't talk to the police, but maybe when he finds out I know he lied to the police, he'll also answer the question of where he lost the knife."

Bailey asked, "Why can't I ask him where he lost it?"

"No way," said Fen.

"All right," said Bailey. "Me and Lou."

Thelma perked up. "You might as well include me. I've been gathering information along with the rest of you."

Fen's head wagged like the tail of a geriatric dog. "I have more years of interviewing suspects than you three put together."

Lou snapped back at him. "Don't be too sure of that. Putting together news stories isn't much different from investigating a crime."

Fen couldn't deny the truth of her words. A skilled reporter used many of the same techniques to pull facts out of people.

Still, he wanted to have the first crack at Riley by himself. "I now have leverage over him because I know he lied to the police."

Lou countered with, "You wouldn't have known that if I hadn't discovered it. He might be more inclined to talk to me. He knows you're a former state trooper and sheriff."

Fen sensed the ground shifting from underneath him, but he wasn't ready to give up yet. "You've already agreed to go to Bastrop tomorrow and verify important information."

"I can leave after we interview Riley. I'll have all day and evening to talk to people in Bastrop."

Fen knew when he'd lost a battle. "All right. I'll call Riley and try to set up a meeting early tomorrow morning. Lou and I will go."

Bailey traded glances with Thelma. The artist whispered something in Thelma's ear. She responded with, "That's a dandy idea."

Bailey squared her shoulders. "We'll agree that you and Lou find out where Riley says he could have lost his knife. After you tell us, we'll take it from there."

Fen narrowed his gaze. "What do you mean, you'll take it from there?"

Thelma lifted her chin. "Bailey and I will find out if it's possible that Riley is telling the truth. You'll be busy all day working with students and we'll be free to snoop."

Fen's gaze fixed on Bailey. "What about your painting?"

"It's finished. So is Cory's. His turned out a lot better than I thought it would. Someone's bound to buy it on Saturday."

Bailey cut Fen off before he could object. "You can always come along behind us if you think we didn't ask the right questions."

Fen rubbed his temples. "You three waited until I was dead on my feet, starving, and suffering from caffeine withdrawal before you ambushed me." He released a huff of exasperation. "You're right about me being busy with students tomorrow. Some of them have a long way to go before their paintings are ready to sell."

Bailey spoke in a soft, pleading voice. "Does that mean we'll all get to help?"

Fen nodded. "Lou's with me tomorrow morning and she'll relay what we learn from Riley. If any leads come out of our conversation, you two will follow up."

Lou finished the conversation with, "Pull out your phone and call him before you forget."

"Oh, yeah. I guess I should do that before you three take over completely."

Ren's voice drifted from the kitchen. "Take over what?"

Fen spoke louder than he intended. "Nothing. You lost a day of painting. You'll spend tomorrow up a ladder."

Chapter Twenty-Seven

I t wasn't often that Fen woke up not feeling well, but this was one of those days. Self-diagnosis told him that yesterday's storm blew in something that triggered his sinuses to flow like the swollen Colorado River. A hot shower and over-the-counter medications were usually enough to head off anything if he didn't delay.

In a move that contradicted his long-established habit of starting each day with coffee, he went from bed straight to his shaving bag and unwrapped two large pills. The label on the box promised immediate relief from anything to do with eyes, nose, throat, and lungs. Following this, he adjusted the water in the shower to something just short of cooking a lobster. After twenty minutes of steam, he could breathe through his nose again.

Once on the mend, he got back to his morning rituals by taking Sally's photo in hand. He told her about the physical ailment and reassured her he'd taken steps to make a quick recovery. Thirty minutes later, the woman in the picture knew all he hoped to accomplish on this day. He took her photo to the porch that connected to his bedroom and they shared a cloudless morning and a glorious sunrise. A therapist might not approve of his obsession to cling to his former wife, but this was his time to spend with Sally as he saw fit.

Back inside, he placed her photo back on his nightstand and made his bed. Before leaving the room, he examined the painting he'd named *Generations*. It still needed a few final touches. He stood back, stared, and allowed the work to speak to him. Something very subtle was missing. He promised himself that tonight he'd spend as much time as it took to discover the missing detail.

Thelma must have heard the steps creak as he came down the stairs. She came through the kitchen door carrying a large glass of orange juice. "Drink this and I'll bring you another. I could tell by the amount of water you used that you're not hitting on all eight. Did you take your sinus-busters?"

"Uh-huh."

"There's coffee if you change your mind." She went to where he sat and placed her palm on his forehead. "At least there's no fever. You may have caught it in time. Make sure you put a handkerchief in your back pocket, just in case."

"It's already there. Thanks."

Lou made her appearance looking fully put together, something that rarely happened before eight in the morning. She was a down-to-earth reporter who wore functional clothes—nice, but not too nice.

Thelma delivered a carafe of coffee to the table and Lou swooped on it like an eagle after a fish. It wasn't unusual for her to not speak until the first wave of stimulant hit her. Half a cup did the trick this morning.

"This place must have a tankless water heater." She looked at Fen. "You spent more time in the shower than a teenage girl getting ready for her first date."

Fen wasn't sure how to respond, so he grunted and took a sip of orange juice.

Lou kept talking. "I've been thinking about how we can get the most information out of Riley without him shutting down. I think the good-cop, bad-cop routine will work the best."

Another grunt that meant nothing.

"I'll be the bad cop. He'll expect tough questions from you. It will throw him off guard if I'm the one grilling him while you play Mr. Nice Guy." She looked at him with expectation painted on her face. "What do you think?"

Fen toyed with the rim of his glass. "Why don't we wait and see how he reacts? He may tell us all we need to know without having to pressure him."

Lou leaned back in her chair with arms crossed. "That's not a plan, it's a nothing. Have you even thought about what you want to ask him?"

"Of course I have. I'm going to ask him if he knows where he might have lost his knife."

Lou hissed. "That's terrible. All he has to say is no. I'll need to lay the groundwork with statements of facts like, 'I know you lost the knife used to kill Lee Grimes. The police have the knife and they intend to use it as evidence against you. Pretend you're a juror, Riley. What would you think?'"

Lou leaned toward him. "This is where you play the good cop and say, 'I believe your story. People lose knives all the time.'"

Lou seemed especially pleased with her plan. "That's where I come back in and say, 'Not every day and not if they carry it in a leather scabbard with a snap to secure the flap.' Then, you say—"

"Breakfast is ready," shouted Thelma as she burst from the kitchen with platters in each hand.

Fen sat up straight. "Sometimes I think I'm eating in a five-star restaurant. I'm not sure why I'm so hungry this morning."

Thelma had the answer. "Probably because you're fighting off a cold. Feed a cold, starve a fever." She launched into a lecture on the medicinal power of eating three balanced meals a day.

Fen silently gave thanks for the meal and the interruption to Lou's rambling plan. He had no intention of following it, but didn't want to get into a confrontation so early in the morning. If he ate slowly, Riley Eastham would arrive before Lou could relaunch her over-thought dialogue.

Minutes later, the ring of the doorbell sounded. Fen had stretched the time it normally took him to finish his meal by taking small bites and discussing the art show.

Lou followed Fen as if she was his shadow. He whispered over his shoulder. "Let's talk to him on the front porch." He cut his eyes toward the dining room and lowered his voice even more. "More privacy."

Lou nodded in agreement.

"Good morning, Mr. Eastham," said Fen as he shook hands. "This is Lou Cooper. She's a newspaper reporter from back home and is here to report on the art fair this weekend."

Riley extended his hand and shook Lou's. "Can we agree to use first names? Smithville folks don't know who you're talking about if you use Mr. or Mrs. They're completely lost if anyone says Ms."

His gaze went from Lou to Fen. "Not only do you have the reputation as one of the top artists in the state, but your one-woman press corps travels with you. That's excellent marketing."

Fen let out a boisterous laugh. Lou didn't.

The sound of another car door slamming caused Fen to look past Riley. Bonnie Sterling rounded her vehicle and walked up the sidewalk. She skipped up the steps and met the other three on the front porch. She explained her presence. "I went to see Sonny in the hospital, but they told me to come back later."

Fen made it a habit to note couples' reactions to each other. They could tell you a lot without words. It wasn't anything Riley said, but what went unsaid that tipped him off. All was not right between Bonnie and her fiancé. While he looked for a diplomatic way to separate the betrothed, Riley came to Fen's rescue.

"Honey, thanks for going to see Sonny, but it was a waste of time. They told me yesterday that they aren't allowing visitors. I should have told you."

"Oh." Her face brightened. "No worries. I'll run along."

Riley looked at Fen. "Tell me if I'm butting in, but you said Lou is here to report on the festival. Correct?"

Lou spoke for herself. "That's right. It's part of the reason—"

Riley spoke over her. "I'm an entrepreneur. That means my mind is always at work thinking of ways to make and sell things that people either want or need. There's a lot of marketing involved." His gaze fixed on Lou. "You're here to report on Fen teaching aspiring artists for a week and then helping them display and sell their works." He took a breath. "Why not do a companion article that tells the story through the eyes of a budding artist?"

Fen spoke before Lou could. "That's brilliant. I've had plenty of articles written about me, but I can't remember reading one from the point of view of one of my students."

Lou sputtered but didn't say no, so Riley turned to his fiancée. "What do you say, honey? You've been chirping all week about how wonderful it is to get tips from an artist of Fen's stature. It would do him a favor and could boost your career, too. It's a win-win situation, and you know how I love those."

Fen noticed the muscles in Lou's jaw flex. Her plan for playing bad cop dissolved like grains of salt in boiling water.

It only made sense that all four wouldn't sit on the porch listening to each other's conversations. Lou's next insult came when Riley suggested the ladies make themselves comfortable inside, while he and Fen contend with any mosquitoes that might happen by the porch. The extra-firm closing of the front door told Fen he needed to put some distance between himself and Lou after he spoke with the fast-talking businessman.

Riley slid into a chair without hesitation or invitation. "I hate keeping things from Bonnie, but I might be in trouble."

"What kind of trouble?" asked Fen.

"The kind that could send me to jail for perjury."

Riley rocked at a fast pace. Fen completed two trips up and back before he asked, "Does your attorney know you're here talking to me?"

"Yes. I lied about one day and my attorney wants us to clear that up. To preempt the prosecution, he wants you to prove where I was through an investigation. I went to Bastrop to explore getting involved in a housing development."

Three more creaks of wood on wood took place before Fen asked. "Was that the only lie?"

"The only one. I have plenty of proof for all the other days."

"Why did you lie?"

"To protect someone at the meeting."

"Ah. The one your server didn't recognize."

Riley's rocking halted as he jerked his head to the right. "You already know. Have you told the police?"

Chapter Twenty-Eight

Fen kept his gaze on the mural across the street. "Instead of discussing what I might, or might not do, why don't we talk about something else? How did you lose your knife?"

Riley unclenched his hands from the arms of the rocker and resumed his quick back-and-forth motion. "I wish I knew. That knife means the world to me."

"Were you in town on the day, or days, before you noticed it missing?"

"My dad wore jeans every day but Sunday when he went to church. He laced his belt through a brown scabbard with a snap on the flap. I inherited his knife and scabbard and I can still hear him say that I'd never lose his knife as long as the snap was good. The snap was weak, but serviceable." He paused. "At least I thought it was. I should have had it replaced, but everything about it reminded me of Dad."

Fen knew this wasn't the answer to his questions, but it gave him insight into the man, which was of equal, if not more, value.

The two men kept rocking, and Riley continued his story.

"I travel often on business, which means I leave the knife at home and wear slacks. Around town, you'll only see me in Wrangler boot-cut jeans. If you see me in jeans, there's a lockblade knife in a brown scabbard on my hip... just like Dad."

He brought his gaze to a squirrel that ventured into the yard. "On the day before I left on a business trip, I ran some errands in town."

"What errands?"

"A trip to the hardware store."

"Are you sure you had the knife on you there?"

"I used it to cut open a package containing a new pair of pliers. The way they package those things, it takes something with a sharp blade to get them out."

Fen held his peace and Riley kept talking. "I then went to get my teeth cleaned."

"In town?" asked Fen.

"Yeah. Dr. Fox's office."

"Could you have lost it there?"

"I called once I realized it was missing. The receptionist checked with everyone in the office. No knife."

"Then where?"

"Grocery store, and home until it was time to go to a city council meeting. I thought it would never end. Mildred Fox had to know every detail of a proposition to purchase new Christmas lights. What should have been a thirty-minute meeting turned into three hours."

"That's a long time to sit. I'd have been lying on the floor snoring at the one-hour mark."

Riley let out a sigh. "The last time that I'm sure I touched my knife was in the cab of my truck after cutting open plastic hard enough to dull the blade. That night, I took my jeans off and left the scabbard with the belt running through it. I didn't realize it was missing until I returned from the business trip and noticed how light my jeans felt."

Fen rose from his rocking chair. Riley followed suit and asked, "What should I tell my attorney?"

"Tell him the police don't know about your trip to Bastrop. I'll sit on that information for the time being. If I discover who killed Lee Grimes, the police have better things to do than come after you because you forgot about a business meeting. If I don't identify the killer, I'll have to tell the police."

Riley gave a worried nod of approval.

Fen held up a hand to show he had one more thing to say. "Tell your attorney I said thanks for the referral to investigate where you were. He must have spoken to Audrey West."

Riley's eyelids widened. "How did you know she suggested it?"

"I didn't until now. Thanks."

It wasn't long before Riley brought his truck to life, turned onto 2nd Street and disappeared as he drove through downtown. Fen sat back in his rocker to process the information. Was Riley's story the whole truth? Probably not, but which parts? Was he lying about losing the knife? His tone and demeanor didn't show deception. Yet, he was a skilled businessman, used to high-stakes negotiations.

Fen's train of thought derailed before he explored the possibilities of who might have found the knife and where. The face of a certain green-eyed city attorney forced its way into his thinking. Why had she contacted Riley's attorney? Was she trying to protect Riley or convict him? Did she already know that Riley had lied to the police and was giving his attorney a heads-up?

"Audrey West," whispered Fen. There were too many things about her that didn't add up. He knew from a computer search that she specialized in family law, but here she was in a tiny town working part-time as the city attorney, occasional cowgirl, and mother to a local cop. Of all the small towns in Texas, she chose this one to move to. Why?

The biggest question of all was why she'd played the game of lover's peek-a-boo with him. Was it to get close to him to gain inside information into the investigation? Perhaps, but there was something more. Something deeper. The opening of the front door put an end to questions without answers. At least for now.

Ren and Bailey came onto the porch, both dressed for a day of painting. The mural artist spoke first, which came as no surprise. "I'll finish today, even if I have to plug in a spotlight tonight."

Bailey asked, "When can we set up our booth?"

"Not until Saturday morning," said Fen.

A shake of Bailey's head told him she didn't like his response. "There's nothing in the rules that says we can't set up our booth tonight. We just can't sell anything before 9:00 a.m. on Saturday."

Fen knew she'd found a loophole in order to score a prime spot. "Call someone from the city and make sure."

"We thought you'd do that since you're tight with a certain city official."

Fen cleared his throat and gave both girls an accusatory stare. He settled his gaze on Bailey after a thought wandered into his mind. "It seems you have too much time on your hands today."

Bailey puffed out her cheeks and released a breath. "Don't worry about me. Cory's keeping me entertained. I hope you realize you've created a monster. Painting is all he can talk about. Since acrylic paint dries fast, he's working on his second masterpiece."

"Does he need to go back to the park, or the road that runs past the park?"

She shook her head. "Photos of various scenes are on his laptop. He'll choose the shot he likes the best and stare at it for two or three hours. Then he'll mix colors like a mad scientist and slap paint on canvas all day and into the night. If he trades his farm supply baseball cap for a beret, I'm looking for a different boyfriend."

A grin pulled up at the corners of Fen's mouth. "That means you'll be able to do research for me today. I need you to go to the local library and see if they have a collection of high school yearbooks. If they don't, go to the school and see if they have back issues. I'll send you a text with instructions for exactly what I'm looking for."

"What about you calling Audrey?"

Fen rubbed his chin, sidestepped her question, and looked at Ren. "Is John working tonight?"

She gave her head a firm shake. "They have him scheduled to work a twelve-hour shift tomorrow. He'll go on duty at 5:00 a.m."

"Good. None of the other artists will be up that early and you can get any spot you want."

Both Bailey and Ren groaned. Ren put words to her thoughts. "That's awful early."

Bailey hooked her arm in Ren's. "Don't worry. I have an idea that will save Fen a phone call and we won't have to get up in the middle of the night."

Fen asked. "Do I want to know what your plan is?"

"It's best you don't."

He thought it best to ignore her comment, and asked, "Who's going to sketch caricatures first?"

Ren raised her hand. "I'll start off."

Bailey tugged her arm. "Yesterday's rain put you way behind schedule. You need to get started. I'll help you set up."

They skipped down the steps and around the corner of the house. The front door opened again and out walked Lou, with Thelma following behind. "I'm off to Bastrop."

Fen held up a hand. "I've been thinking."

He paused a second too long and Lou filled the void with, "It's about time. How close are you to untangling this mess?"

"That depends on whether you, Bailey, and Thelma succeed in each of your assignments today. I think we're close, but things still aren't clear enough." He slapped his hand on his hip. "What I'd give to have eight to ten hours off to paint and think."

"All you have to do is cram a day's teaching into three or four hours. That would give you most of the afternoon and all evening to do that thing you do."

Thelma added, "Ren's going to be up a ladder all day, Bailey's doing whatever you told her to do, and Cory's setting up his easel in the backyard." She thrust her hands into the pockets of her apron. "I wonder how many other painters are going to paint from home?"

Fen lifted his chin. "Thelma, that's brilliant. Yesterday, everyone had to paint from home, or wherever they're staying. I still have time to call all of them and give them the choice of coming here this morning or finishing their work at home. After all, that's the reason they took photos and made sketches. It will save me from driving all over the county."

"Now you're using that head of yours for something more than keeping your ears separated. Don't tell them there'll be warm, chewy cookies if they come here, but say by staying home they'll have more time to paint."

Fen was on a roll and kept talking. "Even if most or all of

them come here, they can spread out in the backyard. I can also give them instructions on their booth setup at one time."

"Heck," said Thelma. "To save time, I might as well feed them sandwiches and chips for lunch. That way, they'll get through even quicker."

Lou looked up at Fen. "I'm still counting on you to pull another rabbit out of your Stetson and give me a story that will blow my hair back."

"If I don't, you can always ride back to Newman County with your window rolled down and your head sticking out the window."

She took off at a quick pace. "Not funny."

Chapter Twenty-Nine

It came as a surprise and a blessing that only half of Fen's students wanted to come to The Katy House to get last-minute tips. Most of the people proved to be extroverts, or those who looked upon their art as a hobby and not a livelihood. After they set up, it soon became obvious that most were quite content with talking. They'd also smear the occasional dab of paint to justify the money spent taking the course.

This suited Fen. For the first hour, he examined each student's work, complimented them on their effort, and pointed to at least one small addition that would bring their work up a notch. He learned a long time ago that success came from implementing tiny, marginal improvements.

Lunch was a boisterous affair with much laughter and self-deprecating humor. There seemed to be an unwritten rule that you could critique your own painting, but not the work of a fellow artist.

Ren climbed down from her ladder and joined the group as they munched on sandwiches and Thelma's cookies. With mouth half-full, she turned to Fen and asked, "Why aren't you working on your painting?"

Everyone overheard her question and barked out words encouraging him to reveal his current work in progress. He resisted, but the group wouldn't take no for an answer. It wasn't long before he returned with an easel and the landscape named *Generations*. The group formed a half-moon and waited for the big reveal.

Gasps, oohs, and ahs sounded when he moved so the gathering could see. Compliments followed, including one that bordered on adoration and another that hinted at jealousy. After the initial jolt, the more serious artists in the group pointed out details that took his painting from the realm of amateur to professional.

A young man wearing a tie-dyed shirt and a multi-colored knit hat asked, "What price will you put on it?"

That was a question that Fen expected. He'd heard it a thousand times over the years and had developed a standard answer. "If I'd painted this when I was in college, fifty dollars. Five years later, when I was a highway patrolman, I'd have sold it for two-fifty. After newspapers and magazines printed stories about me, I'd have sold it for ten times that amount."

"How did you know how to price them at each stage of your career?"

"Great question. You have to build a reputation. That takes patience and hard work in developing your skill and your sales strategy. In the early days, I looked to see what other artists with my skill level were getting for their paintings. That told me what I could reasonably charge." He cast his gaze to eager listeners. "I attribute most of my success to a lucky break when reporters and writers put my name and face out for the public to see. I was an oddity by being an artist-lawman."

A voice came from the left side of the semi-circle. "It wasn't a lucky break." She pointed. "A painting like this takes talent, inspiration, and years of study."

Fen smiled. "That's true, but a little luck along the way also helped."

"You haven't answered my question," said knit cap.

Fen looked at him. "For a work this size and complexity, I'll price it at ten-thousand dollars if I can add the last element without ruining it."

"It looks finished to me."

Fen shook his head. "The title of this work is *Generations*. There are only two generations of tractors. There needs to be at least one more."

"I think less is more," said the scruffy artist. "I'd take the ten grand and move on to the next one."

"You may be right. I'll give your critique careful consideration."

Fen moved away from the painting as the gathering soon divided into opposing camps. One group thought adding anything else to the painting would only detract from what they considered was a finished work. The other group believed art should mirror life. Therefore, three or even four generations of tractors would improve the story of the painting.

Ren sidled up to Fen. "You got them thinking."

"Thinking and feeling, that's why we paint. Do you believe something's missing?"

She stared at the painting. "It needs one more generation, but make it subtle." She then laughed out loud. "Don't ask me how. Subtlety isn't my strong suit."

The rest of the day passed with people putting the finishing touches on their paintings and dispersing, mainly in groups of twos and threes. Fen made sure to tell everyone the schedule for set-up and tear-down of their booths. By two-thirty, the last artist, the man with the knit cap, shook his hand, thanked him, and left.

Fen took his easel and painting to his room. On the way, he spoke to Thelma. "I'm making a do not disturb sign and taping it on my door. What time is supper?"

"Six o'clock."

"Perfect. Tell everyone that I'm not to be disturbed until then."

She flipped her hands in a motion that she might use to shoo away a kitten. "If it's quiet you want, then get up those stairs. We're having stew and a big salad tonight. I already made the stew from leftovers so there's plenty of time for me to nap in the living room. That front door rattles plenty loud when people come in, so I'll make sure you're not disturbed."

Fen asked, "Did you hear anything from the receptionist at the dentist's office about them finding Riley Eastham's knife?"

Thelma shook her head. "My sources let me down. The receptionist there now isn't the same one that was there when Riley might have lost his knife. No one local knows where she moved to."

"What about the dental hygienist who cleaned his teeth?"

"I called her and she said the knife wasn't in that high-dollar chair that tilts back."

"Thanks, Thelma." Fen took a step but stopped and turned. "Are there any rumors going around about why the receptionist left?"

"Too many. Everything from running away with a truck driver to stealing from petty cash. And that's only two of the things I heard."

Fen lifted his straw hat and settled it back on his head. "What does that tell you?"

"If there's over three rumors, then people are making things up. The only way you'll know for sure is to ask the dentist or find the woman who used to work there."

"We already know what the dentist said. She gave no notice and didn't leave a forwarding address."

"That sounds fishy to me," said Thelma. "People don't pack up and leave without a good reason."

Fen thanked her, even though she'd given him another mystery to solve and time was running out. Once in his room, he pulled out his phone and called Lou. She whispered a brief, "Hello."

He lowered his voice to match hers. "Any progress?"

"Yeah. I know who the mystery man is. Do you want to know who?"

Fen spoke the man's name.

"You rat!" said Lou. "You already knew."

"But I needed someone trustworthy to verify it."

"You can't sweet talk your way out of this. You owe me."

"Not yet," said Fen. "But I will if you can find Sue Rangle."

A few seconds passed while Lou mentally matched the name to one found in the thick file completed by the police. "She's the dentist's receptionist who left town."

"Correct. You need to locate her and find out why she left. Thelma tried, but only got rumors on where she went and why."

"Now you have my attention. Any idea of where to start?"

"I'll call Candy. She has a way of going through back channels to get information only the police or federal agencies have access to. Come back here and pack. You may travel tonight."

Lou didn't bother with a salutation.

Fen placed his next call to Candy and explained what he needed. Her response was a brisk, "I'll get on it. Anything else?"

"I need financial statements for half a dozen people for the last six months."

"Text me the names. When do you need them?"

"The sooner the better. I'll be up late tonight."

"Isn't the art festival tomorrow?"

"That's why you have so little time to get the bank records to me."

Candy usually had a better sense of humor. "I don't know who's worse about giving me deadlines, you or Chuck."

"Mine aren't as frequent."

The phone went silent as a wave of partial satisfaction swept over Fen. Things were moving in the right direction, but there were still many gaps to fill. He looked at his painting, and then at his backpack that held his computer and a thick file. The file won out this time. He'd pore through it again, searching for something that would link the murder of Lee Grimes to the assault on Sonny Eastham.

He transformed his bed into an office. Every time he came across the name of a suspect, he jotted their name on a yellow legal pad. He then created a separate pile on the bed of original reports that mentioned the person. There was some overlap, but not as much as he expected. The first three names he came across were Riley Eastham, his fiancée Bonnie Sterling, and Riley's son, Sonny Eastham.

The second group of three were Mildred Fox, her son Clayton, and Audrey West. He felt guilty for including Audrey, but that didn't stop him from following the facts. She'd tried too hard to distract him, and truth be told, she'd succeeded.

Next, he made a pile for the two victims. Sonny's pile intrigued him because he was both a suspect and a victim. As for Lee Grimes, the murder victim, his pile was thicker than the rest. It was obvious the police had delved deep into his past. Perhaps they'd missed something, so Fen took his time and re-read every scrap of information. The thing that puzzled him the most was the note written in Lee's scrawl.

I know about the kid.

Fen put the note back in the file, then set the alarm on his phone for six o'clock. He'd eat supper and spend the rest of the night adding the last element to his painting. At least, that was his plan.

Chapter Thirty

At 6:01 p.m., Fen settled into his chair at the table. Thelma delivered a tureen of stew and individual bowls of salad. She came through the swinging doors of the kitchen again with a platter of hot cornbread and spoke while putting the last dish in front of Cory. "Nothing fancy tonight, but it will keep body and soul together."

Fen gazed at an unoccupied chair. "Where's Lou?"

"She blew in and left before I could fix her a sandwich to take with her. Said she was going to Houston."

Bailey joined the conversation. "I'm glad it's her going to that mosquito-infested swamp and not me. The only thing I took with me from Houston was a few clothes and terrible memories."

"Where's Ren?" asked Fen.

"Cleaning brushes. She finished the mural and it looks great." She changed the subject. "I had to sort of borrow the yearbooks you wanted. They're on the coffee table in the living room."

Fen tilted his head. "'Sort of borrowed' means you took

them without permission. Make sure you 'sort of' take them back after I'm finished with them."

She nodded to show that she would, then asked, "How close are we to solving the case?"

"It's down to receiving a report from Lou, what's in the yearbooks, some financial statements, and me putting everything together." He stabbed a bite of salad. "Are you in a hurry to get home?"

Bailey issued a sound that accompanied a pout. "Cory thinks he should leave by noon tomorrow."

Fen shifted his gaze to Cory and tilted his head as a way of asking him to explain.

"My sergeant called me. He told me I could stay as long as you needed me, but..."

Fen finished the sentence. "He's shorthanded and wants you back as soon as possible." Fen looked into his bowl of stew. "I should have released you to go home when Sonny Eastham got himself shot. He's no longer a threat. Call your sergeant and tell him you can work tomorrow."

Bailey's posture seemed to turn into concrete. "Not tomorrow. He has two paintings to sell."

Fen looked up from his bowl of stew. His mind was so fixed on the details of the case that he hadn't realized how uncaring he sounded.

Bailey pleaded her case and added a personal attack. "You get this way every time we get close to the end. Nothing else matters. Cory came here to protect me and did a great job. His paintings are good enough to sell and he deserves a chance to try."

Cory interrupted. "Fen's right. Sonny's no longer a threat and I should have gone back to Georgetown yesterday. They pay me to be a deputy sheriff, not to paint. I'll call my sergeant and tell him I'm leaving tonight." He looked at the food before him and grinned. "Right after I have one more of Thelma's fabulous meals."

Thelma lifted her chin. "If you're trying to make sure I pack you some cookies to eat on the trip home, it worked."

Bailey hung her head. "This stinks."

Cory placed his hand on hers. "It would help if you'd enroll at Southwestern and get a degree in art. I'm considering taking some classes next semester."

"What classes?"

"I already have an associate's degree. I might as well finish what I started and get a degree in business. I could minor in art."

Bailey's eyes shifted back and forth and her voice softened. "That might work." She tilted her head toward Fen while still looking at Cory. "Fen's been trying to get rid of me ever since he took me in. I can't tell you how many lectures I've heard about going to college. Even Ren is pressuring me to move to Georgetown. She wants us to get an apartment together."

Fen's stomach did a slow roll. He had known the day would come when Bailey would want to leave and make her own way in the world. Little did he know the decision would come in the middle of a murder case. The timing couldn't have been worse. He hadn't dealt with the feelings that would inevitably accompany an empty room over the garage and didn't want to think about it tonight.

Thelma's solid voice rescued him from the moment. "There's a time to talk, a time to make plans, and a time to butter cornbread and eat it while it's hot. Stew isn't good cold, either." She looked at him and winked. Once again, she fulfilled her promise to Sally and took care of him.

Ren blew in through the kitchen. "I'm hungry enough to eat a rhinoceros. What are y'all talking about?"

Fen responded. "Nothing until we finish eating."

"That's fine with me. My dad says that too many words while eating causes indigestion."

The gathering took her father's words to heart and consumed their meal in near silence. As usual, Ren couldn't keep from jabbering between bites. The mural painter didn't seem to possess the capacity to refrain from occasional comments.

While the young people ferried dirty dishes to the kitchen, Fen grabbed two cookies from the platter and gathered the yearbooks from the coffee table. As he climbed the stairs to his room, he wondered what secrets the yearbooks would hold. It took a while to find what he was looking for, but there it was in black and white photos. A major piece of the puzzle slid into place. The case wasn't solved, but it was well on its way. This released him to work on his painting.

Days spent not painting gave his mind a chance to tell him what was missing on the canvas. It turned out to be a third generation in the form of a tractor, the oldest of the three. Instead of showing it as a rusting relic, he placed it out of sight on the far side of the field. A small cloud of black smoke belched from the unseen mechanical beast.

He knew it was a subtle representation of the oldest tractor, but it had to be there to complete the story of three generations.

It surprised him he'd completed the work so fast. The tiny amount of mostly black paint had plenty of time to dry before tomorrow's show.

Finishing the painting invigorated him, and hours remained before he'd turn in for the night. He went back to the mounds of files on his bed and pored through them. Of all the items in the file that stood out to him, the handwritten note from Lee Grimes was the most perplexing. He repeated its words three times. *I know about the kid. I know about the kid. I know about the kid.*

Fen swallowed hard. Could Lee Grimes have discovered the father of Audrey's son? She and her paramour's family had gone to great lengths to conceal the identity of John's father. What if the bumbling criminal from Bastrop had stumbled upon something that would embarrass one of the most influential families in the state? Was Lee trying to blackmail Audrey, and she put a quick end to him? Perhaps all she did was call the family's attorney, and he arranged a killing. Fen hoped Audrey wasn't behind the killing; she had awakened something in him.

He dug through the stacks until he found the notes of his interview with Riley Eastham. He might have lost his knife at an unnecessarily long city council meeting. A meeting attended by Audrey.

A long sigh of regret came from Fen as he saw Riley through the lens of his imagination. The businessman squirmed and shifted his weight in a chair until the weak snap gave way and his father's knife slipped out. Audrey was at the meeting and might have found it on the floor. "No," he whispered. "She's too smart to do it herself."

His mind whirled with possibilities. "Sonny Eastham." The money for that new truck came from somewhere. He could see Sonny selling drugs to make big, fast money. Or was that money a down payment on the Grimes hit job?

His mind shifted back to Audrey. Attorneys who specialize in family law make a very good living. Audrey was raised in the country, which almost guaranteed she was no stranger to firearms. She could have shot Sonny to send a message that he'd be more than sorry if he tried to extort more money from her than she'd already paid him to kill Grimes.

The more he thought about it, the more convinced he was that Sonny killed Lee Grimes.

The painting on the easel in his room caught his eye. Even his art told him that the case involved three generations: John's paternal grandfather, John's father, and John fit what his painting was trying to tell him.

His mind kept grinding away. Chuck and Candy told him to wash his hands of anything that involved John's biological father. Could Audrey have taken care of the problem and not involved the powerful family? This left him asking what he should do about it. On the one hand, Fen had an internal code of ethics that told him to do what was right and let the chips fall where they may. On the other hand, he didn't like the idea of becoming another body found floating in a river.

These were the deepest waters Fen had ever been in. He'd need to be absolutely positive that Audrey paid Sonny Eastham to kill Lee Grimes, and she'd wounded Sonny as a warning to not cross her. With stakes this high, he'd spend a long night going over the files again.

It wasn't long before a previously unanswered question popped into Fen's mind. Why was Audrey living in Smithville? A second question followed on the heels of the first. Why had Audrey pursued a relationship with him? He resolved to find out. He'd ask her.

Chapter Thirty-One

Unable to sleep, Fen showered, shaved, dressed, and was out the front door a few minutes before the eastern sky began its task of pushing back the darkness. He didn't care where his steps took him, as long as it was outside in the cool morning air. It was one of those ambling walks that had no purpose other than to convince his mind to take a break, which was easier said than done.

Before he realized what direction he'd taken, the Railroad Museum appeared in front of him. It resembled a small-town depot for bygone passenger trains. A copse of trees stood to the right of the museum with a decent-sized yard in front of it. A sign caught his eye. He moved toward the stand of live oaks and chuckled. Someone had marked off an area with survey stakes and white twine. Inside the rectangle, they'd planted a hand-painted sign that read, RESERVED FOR FEN MAGUIRE, ART INSTRUCTOR.

Fen moved closer and examined the sign. Not only had Bailey drawn a small caricature of his likeness, she'd initialed it and bought herself an extra hour or two of sleep. Leaning against boundaries came naturally to her. At least she'd committed no illegal acts, unlike the misguided actions of her adolescence in Houston.

A local coffee shop opened at six, which meant Fen could score a cup of dark roast and continue his meandering walk. His steps took him past the *Hope Floats* house. He turned down the gravel road, through the gate, and onto the city-owned lot. He closed his eyes and put his imagination to work. The mugshot of Lee Grimes that he found in the file came into view. So did the mugshot of Sonny Eastham. "Assailant and victim," he whispered as he pictured an alcohol-addled young man, a mean drunk, stabbing an incompetent blackmailer.

With eyes still closed, he tried to imagine Audrey shooting Sonny. The only thing his mind produced was the green-eyed beauty sitting in a rocking chair on the front porch of The Katy House. He was sure that she didn't stab Lee. As for shooting Sonny... he wasn't sure.

He opened his eyes, turned, and walked home. Bailey met him as he walked into the dining room. She tented her hands on her hips. "It's about time. We need to get a move on. You have the booth in your truck."

Thelma made her presence known as she shouted from the kitchen. "Nobody's leaving until after you eat breakfast. I know how you are when you're painting or selling. You both forget to eat or drink anything. It's a wonder you don't keel over."

Bailey took a step toward the swinging doors. "Is it ready?"

The only answer Bailey received was a huff of exasperation.

Fen motioned for Bailey to sit. "Where's Ren?"

"John came by and picked her up for breakfast. She'll meet us at the museum." Bailey lowered her voice. "She's going to tell him thanks for a fun week, but he's not really her type."

Fen leaned into her and whispered. "I think it will be a race to see who dumps the other first."

"You two quit whispering. Anyone with two eyes could see they weren't right for each other."

Bailey raised her voice. "Ren's driving back to Georgetown after we tear down the booth this afternoon. There's some sort of get-together tonight."

Thelma came through the door with a platter of French toast in one hand and a plate piled with bacon in the other. "If they could harness that girl's energy, the power company wouldn't need to plant those fancy windmills everywhere."

Fen and Bailey wasted no time in finishing breakfast. Thelma seemed satisfied that they'd eaten like this might be their last meal of the day. "Leave everything where it is and get to work. I'm looking forward to a full day of peace."

That was all the encouragement Fen and Bailey needed. In less than an hour, their booth was up and stocked. Ren brought a few paintings to sell, but she wanted to earn quick cash by sketching caricatures. As with most events in small towns, sales of paintings were non-existent for the first hour while Ren did a brisk business sketching the cartoonish likenesses of children. She made up for the discounted singles of children by up-selling comical family portraits.

Fen spent the first three hours going from booth to booth, encouraging his students and coaching them in the finer points of pricing and selling their paintings.

When he returned to his tent, Ren needed a break. Bailey took over for her outside the booth and Fen welcomed guests to come inside.

Bailey stopped him before she began her shift of knocking out pencil drawings. "You won't believe who made the first sale."

Fen's shake of his head turned into a nod. "Cory."

"Both paintings. Seventy-five for one and a hundred for the other. A well-dressed couple from Austin bought both. I called Cory, and he screamed like a little girl."

"He had them priced right," said Fen. "Did you coach him on what to charge?"

Her eyes sparkled. "I told him it didn't matter how many hours he spent painting; it was what the market said they were worth that counts. I might have left some money on the table."

Fen brushed away her comment. "He'll learn soon enough that there are highs and lows in the world of an artist. What he needs most is to work on his craft and establish an excellent reputation."

The ringing of Fen's phone marked the end of one conversation and the beginning of another. Lou's name appeared on the screen. Her voice rang with excitement. "I found her and you won't believe what I found out."

"Fen," said Bailey in a strained voice. "Someone's here to see you."

He spun to look. His breath caught in his throat. Two green eyes blinked at him. He allowed his gaze to make a quick trip down to sandals then back up and over shorts and a sleeveless knit top. Fen held up a single hand to the face that seemed to ask, *Don't you have time for me?*

"Lou, are you on the road yet?"

"No. You need to listen—"

"I'm swamped at the booth. Call me back when you clear Houston's traffic."

"That will take over an hour, maybe longer."

He pushed a red circle on the phone's face. His action brought a smile to Audrey's face that seemed to absorb the sunshine and radiate it outward. She asked, "Do you have time to show me something that will take my breath away?"

He wanted to say, *You already have,* but thankfully, his

mouth went dry. All he could eke out was, "Eh... I don't know..."

She hooked her arm in his. "Silly man. I came to see your paintings."

They walked into the twenty-foot by thirty-foot white canvas tent. He explained, "The paintings on the left and back walls are Bailey's and Ren's. Mine are on the right."

"I take it the one on the easel is yours, too." It was a statement, not a question, so he only had to dip his chin.

Audrey took her time working from left to right. She stopped at a portrait Bailey had painted. It showed Sally, holding the reins of her horse with the skeleton of their forever home in the background.

"Who's the model? She looks like a cross between a blond goddess and a rodeo queen."

Fen managed to say, "My late wife. Bailey found the picture in an old photo album and asked if she could use it."

Audrey took two steps forward and examined the painting's details. She took one step back and said, "Her eyes. They reveal deep compassion."

Fen gritted his teeth. "That compassion is what killed her."

"What do you mean?"

"A diseased heart that required a transplant, which worked for a while, but her body eventually rejected it. Sally refused to consider applying for another. She said it wasn't fair to others for her to get two."

Audrey turned to face him. A sheen of tears dulled the sparkle in her eyes. "That's the most selfless thing I've ever heard."

She turned away to examine Bailey's other paintings. Silence prevailed until she got to Ren's. "These four must be from the young lady John had a temporary crush on. They're whimsical and so full of life."

"Just like the artist." Fen took a step toward her. "You don't need to worry about John. Ren's leaving after the show closes this afternoon. She could have stayed another day or two, but she's not."

Audrey walked on and took her time examining Fen's landscapes. She made it all the way down the line, saving the painting on the easel for last. "What an interesting work. It speaks of so many things. There's hard work, struggle, youth, aging, retirement and—"

She stopped in mid-sentence. "My goodness. There's another tractor on the far side of the hill." A shiver coursed through her.

"What do you see?" asked Fen.

"It's not what I see, it's what I feel. The black smoke is ominous and somehow evil." She turned to him. "What did you name this?"

"*Generations.*"

She turned back to the painting and spoke as if he wasn't there. "How appropriate."

Bailey came through the opening. "Ren's back. I'm still full from breakfast, so you can grab something or take a break."

Audrey bypassed Fen and stood in front of Bailey. "I'd like to purchase two paintings, please."

"Sure. Which ones?"

"The self-portrait of Ren wearing a clown costume and the amazing portrait you painted of Fen's wife, Sally. You captured her eyes perfectly."

"I cheated a little on that. I copied the eyes from the portrait Fen painted of her. The original looks much better than mine."

Fen cleared his throat. "Audrey and I are going to grab a bite to eat. Wrap up the paintings and make out a ticket."

Fen walked at a steady clip, even though he wasn't sure

where he was going. He looked straight ahead as he said, "I revealed quite a bit about me today. Now I have questions for you."

"Ask away."

"Why did you move to Smithville?" He glanced over in time to see the muscles in her jaw tighten. She laced her arm through his.

They walked together in lockstep as he waited for her to answer his question. Instead, she looked around then brought her gaze back to him. "You already know a lot about me. What you're asking for is a front porch conversation. I'll answer your questions as best I can, but not here, and not now. Would you rather sit in the rockers on my front porch this evening or at The Katy House?"

Fen sensed he needed a home-field advantage. "Let's make it The Katy House."

"I thought that's what you'd say. It needs to be after supper."

"Why?"

"I have a strong inclination that Thelma doesn't enjoy single women putting their feet under her table, especially those anywhere close to your age."

Politeness said he should tell her she was wrong, but memories of the first time he invited Lou Cooper to the house prevented it. To keep the peace, they had dined on the patio that evening. After three steps, he agreed to a meeting at The Katy House after supper. A conversation on the porch would save him many hours of verbal and non-verbal grief from his well-meaning housekeeper.

"If you don't mind," said Audrey, "I'll pick up the paintings tonight. You need to get back to your booth." She turned and was gone without another word.

Chapter Thirty-Two

Gathering clouds brought relief from the intense afternoon sun. Rumbles of thunder in the distance sent the gazes of patrons and vendors skyward. A wall of black approached from the northwest. Fen, Bailey, and Ren wasted no time in backing their trucks to the curb to load their unsold paintings into special racks. With that task complete, they hurried to dismantle the booth, fold it, and slide it into the bed of Fen's truck. Easels, tables, folding chairs, and everything else needed for a weekend sale filled in the gaps. The locking camper shells ensured a waterproof home for the traveling businesses, and not a moment too soon.

The first sprinkles fell at 4:05 p.m., followed by a cloudburst that soaked anyone who'd not heeded the thunder's warning. Fen sat alone with his thoughts in the cab of his truck as Bailey and Ren drove away. He didn't like the way his time with Audrey ended. There were important things they both needed to say, but so far today, timing and circumstances had conspired against them. Hopefully, tonight would go better and he would get some answers.

Without thinking, his hand made a simple motion and the truck came to life. With the windshield wipers slapping the sheets of water aside, he eased away from the curb. After the brief trip back to the bed-and-breakfast, he parked behind Lou's Camry. Holding a rain poncho over his head, he quick stepped to the front porch. Leaving the poncho on the swing and his wet boots on the porch, he opened the door into the welcoming foyer.

It didn't take him long to realize he'd stepped in the proverbial doggy-pooh—again. He felt the chill of Lou's icy stare before he crossed the threshold of the living room.

"Did you forget to charge your phone?" she demanded.

"Uh, no."

"Did you forget we're here to solve a murder?"

This time, he answered with a simple shake of his head.

"Were you taken captive by aliens? Or perhaps a green-eyed attorney hypnotized you?"

"No aliens," said Fen in a weak voice. "Sorry. I should have called you back. What did you find out?"

Lou stood. "Since you believe this isn't really time sensitive, I should make you wait until you read about it in the newspapers or see the story on YouTube."

Fen stayed silent and engaged in a stare-down with the angry reporter. She looked away first, but came back at him with, "If I didn't know this would make a difference in the case, I'd keep it to myself."

Fen motioned for her to sit in one of the two identical chairs in front of the window overlooking the porch. He occupied the other and said, "Tell me. What did Dr. Fox's former receptionist say?"

"Nothing until after I called Candy."

Fen's mouth hinged open. "Why did you call Candy?"

Lou huffed. "The woman slammed the door in my face. I

wanted to report what happened to *someone* who'd tell me what to do next."

He closed his eyes and counted to five. He would have made it ten, but she had every right to be angry with him. With eyelids open, he asked, "What did she tell you to do?"

"To go somewhere, get something to eat, and wait for her to call me back. The reporter in me told me I should stay within sight of the woman's apartment so that's what I did. About forty-five minutes later, a black SUV pulled up and two guys wearing dark suits got out. They went to her apartment and she let them in. Twenty minutes later, they left, and Candy called me back. She said the woman changed her mind and would talk to me."

Fen was processing the story when Lou asked, "What do you know about Candy? Who is she that she can snap her fingers and suddenly a woman who wouldn't give me the time of day is ready to tell me her life story?"

Fen knew his answer wouldn't satisfy Lou. "I've had my suspicions about Candy and Chuck for a long time. He told me I'd find nothing if I tried to dig into his or Candy's past. I took his advice and I suggest you do the same."

A look of frustration came over Lou. "Do you know how hard it is for me to not follow up on leads?"

"Candy and Chuck are the source of our leads. They feed cases to me and I include you and Bailey in the investigations. Be content with what they're doing." He took a breath. "Tell me what the woman said."

"She found the knife that killed Lee Grimes in Dr. Fox's dental chair. Mildred Fox came into the practice as she carried it to her desk. Mildred said she'd return the knife to Riley East-ham. Two days later, Dr. Fox's mother paid her a substantial amount of money to leave town and never mention the knife to anyone."

Fen stood. "This puts an interesting spin on the case. Have you sent me a report yet?"

"Thanks to heavy traffic, I didn't arrive until thirty minutes ago."

Fen turned toward the stairs. "I'll be in my room until it's time for supper."

His feet may have plodded up the stairs, but his mind raced. In his wildest dreams, he hadn't imagined Mildred Fox being involved in the murder of Lee Grimes. Perhaps she wasn't. What happened to the knife after Mildred retrieved it from the former receptionist?

Evidence and responses from interviews were supposed to bring clarity to investigations. The waters of this one remained murky, like the Colorado after today's deluge.

Fen examined the stacks of paper on his bed and sighed. He'd read them so many times he'd reached the point of complete saturation. Instead of poring over them again, he walked into the bathroom and shut the door behind him. He then pulled off his sweat-stained clothes and allowed the shower to assault his head and body.

The cool water helped but didn't unburden him from the sensory overload. Only sleep would help. He dried, put on sleep shorts and a T-shirt, then lay on top of the bed. The ceiling fan clicked out a monotonous beat that became the adult version of a child's lullaby.

He roused when he heard a soft knock on his door and Thelma saying, "Mr. Fen, you have company waiting for you on the front porch." A jumbled dream took flight.

He forced his eyes to open. "I'm coming," he croaked as he pulled both hands down his face and threw his feet over the edge of the bed. He found his footing and went into the bathroom to splash water on his face and survey the carnage caused by going to sleep with damp hair. He determined that only a hat would help.

Since time was ticking away, he settled for rinsing with foul-tasting mouthwash and slipping jeans over his sleep shorts. He didn't realize he was barefoot and had forgotten to grab a hat until he was on the front porch.

Audrey took one look at him and tented her eyebrows. She approached, ran a hand through his tousled hair, and spoke. "You're the most self-confident man I've ever met."

He countered her words by overwhelming them with a string of babbling sentences. "I apologize for my appearance. It's the result of poor time management. I was up most of the night reviewing the two crimes then got up before dawn. Like a fool, I started my day with a long walk. After helping to set up our booth and checking with the students, I must have walked ten miles today, then we went to lunch, and..."

His litany came to an abrupt stop when she placed an index finger on his lips to shush the flow. "You saw what I looked like after a day of working cattle. I'd say we're even."

He lowered his voice. "Not exactly." He wanted to take back the words and add to them at the same time. He couldn't imagine Audrey looking anything short of fabulous. She rescued him by sitting in a rocking chair and saying, "Let's rock and watch it rain for a few minutes before we talk."

Once again, he had the impression that she read his mind. He also recognized she knew exactly when to push and when to pull back. Instead of rushing to confront her with evidence that seemed to implicate her in the crimes, he waited for her to make the first move.

Minutes passed as their chairs once again locked into an identical rhythm. As expected, she broke the silence, not with a question, but with a statement. "You think I'm involved in the crimes."

Fen kept rocking. "There's a lot of evidence that suggests you could be."

"I know." She then stated the reasons like they were items on a shopping list. They were the same ones he'd written the previous night.

Audrey then asked, "Have you discovered any additional evidence today?"

"Yes."

"Do you still think I might be the killer or an accomplice?"

"I haven't had time to process the new information."

She stopped rocking. "Will you have me arrested if you believe the evidence shows I'm involved?"

"Yes."

She started rocking again, but their chairs were no longer in unison. Awkward minutes passed. This time, he broke the silence. "I asked you earlier today why you moved to Smithville. Your answer may help convince me of your innocence."

Audrey gripped the arms of the rocker and pushed up. "Since I'm under investigation, my advice to myself as an attorney is to say nothing. Good night, Sheriff Maguire."

Fen stood. "Good night, counselor. We'll talk again soon."

"Oh?"

"Tomorrow. I'll do my best to look more presentable, but I can't promise that. There's another sleepless night in my immediate future."

Back inside, he went to the dining room where Thelma waited for him. "Are you hungry?"

"Light snacks only. Meat, cheese, and fruit."

"You want thinking foods. What about a pot of coffee?"

"You read my mind."

Thelma opened her mouth to say something else but closed it.

"Say what's on your mind," said Fen.

"All right, I will. Does that green-eyed beauty have you twisted in knots?"

Fen considered how to answer. "I'm used to riding alone in my truck or with Bailey. We both know she won't always be there. When that time comes, if you think I'm too lonely, you can get me a puppy."

"A dog?" Thelma's eyes ping-ponged back and forth as she considered the suggestion. "That could work for a while as long as it stays outside and doesn't keep me up all night barking."

Fen knew engaging him in a new battle of wits was a ploy to get his mind off of Audrey. "If I ever get a dog, it will come into the great room, stay in my bedroom, and watch me paint in my studio. And he'll stay out of your kitchen."

Thelma took her time considering his rules before she added a last condition. "If it tracks in mud, you know where the broom and mop live."

The threat was as hollow as a discarded plastic Easter egg. They both knew that Thelma would never allow Fen to clean the home's floors. She took too much pride in her work.

With negotiations for a potential companion complete, Fen went to his truck and retrieved his latest painting. It hadn't sold, which suited him fine. He believed the work hadn't revealed all its secrets to him.

Chapter Thirty-Three

Once in his room, Fen limited his study to only the newest information received. He read, and reread, Lou's report on Mildred Fox's highly questionable actions in paying a receptionist to move from Smithville and not discuss why. At last, he knew where and how Riley Eastham lost his knife. He played the mental game of *it could be*.

After an hour of concentration, the why still eluded him and the who could be one of multiple suspects.

His focus shifted to the purloined yearbooks from the local high school. Another hour passed before a single photo caught his attention. It was the love-struck look on the faces of a senior boy and a young woman of exceptional beauty. She was in the class a year behind the young man, who was a current person of interest.

Fen noticed a magnifying glass on the table between the two chairs in front of the bedroom window. He retrieved it and meticulously examined every photo in the two yearbooks. Two faces in a crowd of other students appeared in multiple photos. Their eyes spoke of a close relationship.

Next on Fen's agenda was to review his truncated discussion with Audrey. He failed miserably in obtaining any useful information from her. His painting once again caught his eye and he whispered "*Generations.*" Looking down at a closed fist, he unfurled his thumb and said, "John West, youngest generation." His forefinger came next. "Audrey West and the son of someone very important, middle generation." His middle finger formed a trinity. "Someone important enough to scare Candy and Chuck, oldest generation."

His gaze centered on the smoke rising from the unseen tractor behind the hill in the painting. He took in a full breath then expelled it as if trying to disperse the black cloud. Needless to say, the dark puff remained on the canvas and no revelation came.

Desperation fell on Fen. He leaned *Generations* against the side of the bed, then sat on one of the twin chairs. The different angle was enough to make him stare. He tried tilting his head from one side to the other, like a confused puppy. He lost all sense of time as he stared deeper and deeper into what the logical side of his brain told him was only an illusion created by paint on a flat surface. The creative part of his brain told him to keep looking.

On this rain-soaked night, art won. Revelation came without the noise of the lightning strike that felled half a tree in front of the B&B. Fen wondered what had kept him from seeing what was now so clear.

Without thinking, he grabbed his phone and punched in a number. A sleep-strained voice answered. "I'm too close to retirement to chase anyone in the rain."

"You're right Ben, that's why you don't have to do anything until tomorrow."

"Have you looked at a clock lately? It is tomorrow."

"Oh... Sorry. Go back to bed. I'll email you the names of the people I need you to round up and have at The Katy House tomorrow afternoon. You're going to end your career in style."

"Right now, I wish it had ended yesterday."

A SENSE of anticipation settled over the bed-and-breakfast as Fen walked with chest out and took his seat at the head of the table. Thelma placed a platter of scrambled eggs between Bailey and Lou before she gave him a closer look. She spoke in a tone suited for someone with a secret to reveal. "Don't look now, ladies, but the rooster is strutting this morning. I'd say he's solved the case."

Lou reached for her phone. "Don't start until I can record what you say."

Fen responded with, "There's no rush. The guests of honor won't be here until late this afternoon. That will give you plenty of time to put cameras in the living room. Everything needs to be recorded. I'm hoping to get a confession or two to add to the evidence."

"That's awesome," said Bailey. "I have a new spy camera I'd like to try out." She fidgeted in her chair. "What else do you want us to do?"

"Thelma, Lou—I want you to stay out of sight. You can monitor from upstairs. Bailey—I want you downstairs, but out of sight, especially as everyone is arriving. I might need something, but I don't want you getting hurt. There should be nine people in the living room, but not all of them will be seated."

"How many cops?" asked Bailey.

"Two, with more outside."

Thelma asked, "Are you expecting trouble?"

"Expect? No. But it's best to prepare."

She looked at Lou and Bailey. "That means he's keeping his back against a wall and will have his pistol on him."

Lou asked, "Will the story make the front page?"

"It depends on how I play my cards." Fen reached for the eggs. "We'd better eat these before they get cold."

Bailey asked, "Can I pack and leave tonight? I took orders for two portraits and want to get started on them."

Fen gave his head a nod. "I don't see why not. I may need to stay an extra night, but everyone else can go back to Newman County."

Lou said, "When I leave depends on the big show-down this afternoon. I hope there's enough story to fill multiple articles."

"I can't promise you that," said Fen.

Lou let out a huff. "What can you promise?"

Fen spread homemade jelly on a biscuit. "The person who killed Lee Grimes, and the one who shot Sonny Eastham."

Lou's eyebrows drew together. "Why do I have the feeling you're holding something back from us?"

Fen's only response was, "Please pass the salt and pepper."

Chapter Thirty-Four

Ben Crump arrived fifteen minutes early. He came bearing news. "Mildred Fox refused to come until I told her Audrey would be here."

"What about Clayton?"

"Same story. Mother and son are coming together. You can expect Audrey to be all business. She seemed defensive when I spoke to her."

"Like she was hiding something?"

Ben lifted his shoulders and allowed them to fall. "I haven't figured out my wife yet, let alone Smithville's city attorney."

"What about the others?"

The ringing doorbell ended the conversation. Fen strode into the foyer, motioning for Bailey to hide around the corner. He opened the door to admit Riley Eastham and Bonnie Sterling. Fen welcomed Riley with a handshake and smiled at Bonnie. "Please come in and make yourselves comfortable."

Instead of sitting, Bonnie walked a straight line to Fen's *Generations* painting. She studied it like a diamond cutter would examine a large gemstone. "So many people were commenting on this. I can't believe it didn't sell."

"I priced it so it wouldn't," said Fen. "It's an old sales trick. I marked this painting at twice the price it should sell for. That created buzz. Now, I wait for someone with deep pockets to come along who believes they can't live without it. Then I can sell it at a big discount and everyone's still happy."

Riley gave a nod of approval and looked at his fiancée. "Listen to him, honey. Things are worth what people will pay for them."

"That means my painting of the river was worth eighty-five dollars for a week's work."

Fen had another explanation for the modest return. "It wasn't your level of skill, but a lack of patience. You sold it before nine in the morning. People like to look at art before they buy."

A girlish laugh tinkled from Bonnie. "I used all my patience waiting for Riley to set the date for our wedding."

Riley added, "We fixed that problem."

Ben asked, "When's the big day?"

Riley threw out his chest. "Yesterday."

Bonnie's words flowed in a burst of excitement. "That's why I sold the painting so early in the day. He surprised me with a better offer. My wonderful husband arranged for a small ceremony in the backyard. It was perfect."

"Almost," said Riley. "Sonny showed up drunk and passed out before the ceremony. Looking back, we counted it as a blessing. We left him in bed and everyone went to Winchester. We feasted on steaks and danced until our feet ached."

"How cool," said Bailey. Ben and Fen also expressed their congratulations but with more traditional words.

The doorbell sent Bailey scurrying again. Mildred Fox entered with her son and Audrey in tow. The aging matriarch soon blanketed the warmth of the moment with a frosty gaze. "Whoever is responsible for this meeting needs to know I don't appreciate having my day of rest interrupted."

Fen stood his ground. "I'm responsible for calling you here and I make no apologies. My entire week of teaching students suffered after I was summoned to help solve a murder. Then one crime turned into two. Mrs. Fox, I believe you complained about the results the local police had achieved and demanded an outside investigation. Isn't that correct?"

"Their incompetence was on display for all to see, and I don't like the tone of your voice."

Fen shrugged. "You'll like it even less before this meeting is over."

Three loud knocks on the front door interrupted what promised to be a duel of words. Bailey shot from the room. John, dressed in his patrolman's uniform, pushed a handcuffed Sonny Eastham in front of him.

"Put him in the chair in front of the pocket doors," said Fen. "Is he drunk?"

John shook his head. "Hung over."

Fen moved in front of Sonny, looked down on him, and asked, "Head hurt?"

"Leave me alone."

"Not today. I have a story to tell you and you're going to listen."

"I want a lawyer. This boy with a gun arrested me without cause."

Fen noticed Audrey sat on the very edge of her seat. He turned his gaze to John, who'd stationed himself behind Sonny. "Is he under arrest?"

"I told him he was being detained, not under arrest."

Ben moved to look down at Sonny. "If you'd like, I'll arrest you for being drunk in public. The way you reek of booze, you're bound to have enough residual in you to fail a blood test."

Fen knew Ben was bluffing. Sonny must have, too, so Fen nodded to Bailey. She spoke in a calm voice. "Is it too late for me to file charges on him?"

"What for?" demanded Sonny.

"Assault. Don't you remember forcing me against the railing at the river? You had no right to touch me like you did. It was gross. If that man in the boat hadn't come along, there's no telling what you'd have done."

Riley put steel in his words as he stared at his son. "Is that true? Did you try to force yourself on this young woman?"

Sonny slumped in his chair. "Look at her. She's a tease. I know a set-up when I see one."

Fen looked at Audrey. "Counselor, could you define assault for Sonny?"

"Any form of malicious touching or contact. However, this may rise to a higher level than simple assault. From the little I've heard, this could be a felony."

Mildred spoke as Sonny sat looking befuddled by Audrey's grim prediction. "Congratulations, Mr. Maguire. You'll rid the city of a drunk. What about solving the murder?"

Fen turned to face her. "Sonny's not just a drunk, Mrs. Fox. He's a special kind of drunk, a mean one. Everyone reacts differently when under the influence. He loses control."

A look of confusion swept across her face when Fen approached his painting and asked, "Mrs. Fox. What do you think about this work?"

She looked at it and said, "I don't care for it."

"Why not?"

"It's silly and unsophisticated."

"Unlike the portraits in your home?"

"Yes. I can see why your landscapes appeal to some people, but I consider a plowed field with two tractors unimaginative."

Fen accepted the criticism without comment and moved on. "I thought the portrait of your son's former wife to be exceptional. It seemed to hold a place of honor in your home."

Mildred lifted her chin. "She was the perfect daughter-in-law."

He nodded his agreement. "It was such a shame she died before leaving you a grandchild."

A wave of silence descended on the room. Fen pivoted the conversation back to his painting. "The title of this work is *Generations*. I didn't know how appropriate it was until last night. All along, this case was about generations. I've met several families with multiple generations in Smithville. I started asking myself if it's possible there are three generations from the same family involved in the murder of Lee Grimes?"

He paused. "I'm getting ahead of myself. Let's clear one thing up before we continue. Riley Eastham had nothing to do with killing Mr. Grimes."

Mildred demanded, "What about the fact that his knife is the murder weapon? How do you explain that?"

"I'll get to that in due time. But first, both crimes in this case revolve around a note found among Lee Grimes' belongings as much as the knife does. The note reads, 'I know about the kid.'"

He pointed to the canvas. "That leaves us with what this painting depicts—three generations." He pointed to the new tractor, then to the older one, and finally to the black smoke behind the hill. "I know the last tractor is rather obtuse, but that's the way art often is."

Audrey gave him a wicked stare. "If this is going where I think it is, I caution you to be very careful with your words."

Fen straightened his spine. "I appreciate your concern, but

I'm following the evidence, wherever it leads." He turned back to his painting. "Where was I? Oh yes. Generations. It seems Lee Grimes somehow stumbled across a bit of information that a family, perhaps a prominent family, didn't want revealed. He practiced writing what would become a phrase he later used in a letter sent to someone here. The phrase was *I know about the kid.*"

Fen stood in front of Clayton Fox and asked, "Did you ever receive a letter with that phrase in it?"

"Absolutely not."

"I thought you'd say that."

Fen spun to face Bailey. "Do you have the yearbooks?"

From her place in the doorway leading to the foyer, all Bailey had to do was take two steps to retrieve them.

Fen had marked all the pages that showed photos of a young Clayton Fox and a striking blond. He thrust the book at the dentist. "This yearbook is from your junior year in high school. Take your time to look at all the pages marked."

Bailey delivered two magnifying glasses. "Here's one for you and one for your mother. You can look together."

After viewing several pages, Clayton slammed the yearbook shut. "So what, I had a crush on a girl in high school."

Bonnie had remained quiet up to this point. "Who's the girl?"

"That's not important," said Mildred.

Fen shook his head and thrust the second yearbook into Clayton's hand. "This is from your senior year when you were voted the most likely to succeed, among other things. There's no need to look for pictures of your girlfriend in this one. You completed your senior year and graduated, while she and her family left town. However, I suspect there was more than an innocent crush between you and this lovely young woman."

Mildred raised her voice. "Her father took a job in Dallas and the family moved. So what?"

Audrey folded her hands on her lap. "I warned you before, Mr. Maguire. One more veiled accusation of impropriety and we're leaving."

Fen snapped back. "I couldn't care less about impropriety. Especially for something that happened so many decades ago." He paused. "Unless it helps solve these two cases."

He sucked in a full breath. "What I do care about is murder and people who try to hide evidence."

Audrey stood. "Mildred, Clayton, we're leaving. Mr. Maguire is out of his depth and confusing facts with fiction."

Ben took a step forward. "Counselor, you're free to leave, but I'm detaining Mrs. Fox and Dr. Fox. As a courtesy, I'll not handcuff them unless they try to leave."

Mildred's green eyes flashed with anger. "How dare you!"

Clayton attempted to console her. "Now, Mom. Remember your blood pressure. Let Audrey handle this."

Sonny used Ben's concession of not handcuffing Mildred to ask for equity. "These handcuffs are pulling my stitches. If you're not going to cuff the others who are detained, I shouldn't be either."

Ben complied but not before issuing a firm warning of what would happen to Sonny if he tried anything.

Chapter Thirty-Five

F en squared his shoulders and said, "Generations," bringing everyone's attention back to him. "Generations of pride and an obsession to control. These are what eventually led to murder."

Audrey gave her head a shake that telegraphed sympathy. "I thought you were confused. Now, I see you're so dedicated to art that you're finding suspects in your paintings. That doesn't come as a surprise. You're one of many eccentric artists who have lost touch with reality."

"If it's reality you want, it's reality you'll get." Fen pointed an accusatory finger. "Clayton Fox fathered a child when he was in high school and Mildred's husband found jobs for the girl's parents in Dallas."

Audrey held up her hand. "Stop!"

Fen lowered his voice a decibel, taking some of the bite out of his words. "Alright, Counselor. If you don't like the past, let's stick to this year. Either Mildred Fox or Clayton Fox received a letter from Lee Grimes saying he knew about the child."

A small gasp escaped from Mildred.

Fen's gaze shifted from Audrey to Mildred. "It doesn't really matter which one of you received the letter. The bond between mother and son can be very strong, as I believe it is with the two of you. I suspect there are no secrets between you."

"Prove it," said Clayton.

"Gladly. The police have a sworn statement from your former receptionist. She says your mother paid her the equivalent of two years' wages to move back to Houston and not mention finding Riley's knife in your dental chair. She also states she gave the knife to your mother."

Mildred demanded. "She's lying."

"Bank records tell a different story."

A hush fell over the room but didn't last long as Fen turned to face Sonny. "This is your chance to help yourself. Who shot you?"

He opened his mouth, but slammed it shut.

Fen had to give him a reason to speak. "I have to give credit where credit is due, Sonny. Not squealing on Dr. Fox is something very few people would do. He must have terrified you."

Sonny grinned but said nothing.

"How many truck payments did he promise you?"

Fen knew he was on the right track, but Sonny needed a harder push before he'd talk. "Look at Dr. Fox. He's going to say you were the brains behind Lee Grimes writing the extortion letter. He'll deny shooting you, and who's going to believe the word of an alcoholic ex-con against such an upstanding citizen?"

Sonny's eyes scanned the floor as if the answer might appear to him.

Fen gave another verbal shove that he hoped would send Sonny over the edge. "Dr. Fox is also going to say that you killed Lee Grimes. If you go back to prison, it will be on a murder-for-hire charge. You're looking at a life sentence."

That caught Sonny's attention. He stiffened and sat up straight. "I won't grow old and gray in prison."

Fen threw him a tiny lifeline. "I don't believe you intended to kill Lee, only scare him. I bet you'd been drinking to get your courage up. When he saw the knife and came at you, things got out of hand. Those are mitigating factors, but you'll need to cooperate with the police and district attorney for that to make a difference."

Wide, bloodshot eyes stared at Fen. "How'd you know how everything went down?"

A gasp came from Bonnie. Fen glanced at the newlyweds. Riley's head shook from side to side as he listened to his son's confession.

Fen brought his gaze back to Sonny. "Did Dr. Fox shoot you?"

Sonny balked again, so Fen came at him from a different angle. "You're not in prison, so that so-called code of honor among inmates doesn't exist. Besides, I already know he did. He may not be a medical doctor, but he's very familiar with the human body. The shot was too well-placed. He wanted to scare you and it worked. You're still too afraid and stupid to realize how he set you up. That's because you're a silly boy, not a smart man."

Sonny was on his feet. "I'll talk, but not to you or anyone in this room. I'm prison-smart and tough enough to make it on the inside. I know how to bargain for years off a prison sentence."

Mildred, probably out of arrogance, picked the wrong moment to speak. "That's enough. We all heard him confess to killing that man. Everything else is a pack of lies."

Sonny straightened his posture. "You silly old cow. I may go back to prison, but not before I make a deal with the district attorney. Who's more to blame for killing Lee Grimes? The poor alcoholic who couldn't find steady work, or the rich dentist who didn't want his reputation damaged? If I'm going back, I'm taking Dr. Fox with me." He gave a sadistic chuckle. "Who knows, if you don't keel over from a heart attack, you may get to enjoy prison food, too."

Mildred snorted. "I refuse to converse with scum like you."

Fen focused on Sonny and took the bite out of his words. "At least you got to ride around in a new truck for a few months."

"Of all the things I'm going to miss, that truck is at the top of the list."

Footfalls sounded on the stairs leading to the second floor. Lou appeared with a camera in hand. She launched into Clayton and his mother with a barrage of questions.

Dual conversations brought confusion into the room. Fen should have seen it coming. Sonny wasn't ready to face leaving his truck behind. He gave John a shove and threw open the pocket doors that led to the dining room. His flight to freedom lasted all of three seconds. He took one step into the dining room and, *Thwack!* He stumbled back into the living room, hand over his nose. Thelma stood over him with her trusty cast-iron skillet in hand.

Blood cascaded from Sonny's nose onto his shirt.

"Don't you dare get blood on the furniture," shouted Thelma as she took off her apron and threw it at him.

John reached for handcuffs as Ben came to assist. Once they had Sonny secured, Ben said, "Take him back to the hospital."

Lou abandoned the dentist and his mother, choosing to station herself outside to catch John coming through the front door with Sonny.

Ben moved to stand by Fen. "That was more excitement than I expected."

"Don't you want to cuff Dr. Fox and have your picture on the evening news?"

"I'll leave that for the local police. The paperwork from this will take days. Then there will be the trials. Are you sure you did me a favor?"

An officer informed Mildred she was under arrest and told her to put her hands behind her back. She let out a string of words that could take the bark off a tree as the officer recited the Miranda warning. Everyone, including Audrey, received a tongue-lashing.

A second set of handcuffs clicked on Clayton Fox's hands as he was also informed of his right to remain silent.

Audrey was the only person to respond. "I'm sorry, Mrs. Fox, but there's nothing I can do to stop them from arresting you." She spoke to Mildred's back as the officer led her outside. "Say nothing. I'll call a top defense attorney I know. She'll have you out on bail in the next day or two."

Riley Eastham came and stood before Fen and asked, "How much time will Sonny have to serve?"

Fen pulled a hand down his face. "I'm wrong every time I make a prediction about what will happen in a courtroom. Sonny has what they call jail-house smarts. He knows how the system works and is prepared to have his attorney cut a deal."

Bonnie's tear-filled eyes told him she wanted more.

Fen sighed and relented. "My best guess is that he'll be older and wiser when he's released from prison, and you two will still be around to welcome him home."

Bonnie hugged him. "Thank you. We won't give up on him."

Riley tilted his head. "Why didn't you divulge that Clayton

Fox and I were planning to become partners in a housing development?"

"Ah," said Fen. "The business meeting in Bastrop."

"Yeah. Word got back to me that a reporter was asking a lot of questions about who was present."

"Two reasons," said Fen. "It had no direct bearing on either crime." He glanced at Audrey, who'd returned to her seat. "Second, Mildred would consider it the worst betrayal possible by her son. It may kill her if she finds out."

Riley and Bonnie shook his hand and left. Ben followed suit.

Bailey was next to speak. "I'm loading my truck and hitting the road. Thanks for including me. It was more intense than I thought it would be."

Fen received a firm hug and whispered, "Be careful."

Thelma had a look of self-satisfaction on her face. "Aren't you glad I ignored what you said and brought this skillet?"

He gave his head a nod. "You win this round."

Thelma hummed a jaunty tune as she returned to the kitchen. This left only him and Audrey in the living room. She stood, flattened an imaginary wrinkle from her blouse, and gazed at him through misty green eyes. "I'm trying to decide how much to hate you."

"Cases like this make me wonder the same thing."

Audrey snatched her purse from the floor and strode out of the room. The slam of the front door reverberated through the house, sounding very final to Fen's ears.

Chapter Thirty-Six

Displaced covers gave evidence of Fen's thrashing. The bed that had given him such peaceful sleep back in June had failed him during this trip. Or had he failed himself by having his mind so plagued by distractions?

He knew he needed to trade emotion for motion, so he trundled off the bed, stood, and stretched. Coffee and time with Sally came next. It was a ritual he didn't intend to break today or in the foreseeable future.

He made his way down the stairs and stopped at the coffee station. Thelma's voice rang out. "Real coffee is in the carafe. Fill your mug and have your time with Sally. Your breakfast will be ready in forty-five minutes."

"Make it an hour. We have a lot to talk about."

The talk was decidedly one-sided, but the result was surprisingly pleasant. He'd spoken his heart to Sally, and peace awaited him in the shower.

Following breakfast, he went to the front porch as Thelma cleaned the kitchen and made sure The Katy House looked the same as when they arrived. Fen tried to help until she told him to find a place where he wouldn't be underfoot. He chose the front porch.

A familiar vehicle parked behind his truck. Audrey approached, wearing a gray skirt with matching blazer over a white blouse. She wore her hair pulled back, showing off the contours of her face and puffy emerald-green eyes. Fen pushed up from his rocking chair. "I wasn't sure if you'd come."

"I had to flip a coin to help me decide."

"How many times?"

That earned the makings of a smile. "Only three." She sat in the chair next to the one he'd occupied and rocked.

He settled next to her. It didn't take long before they were in sync.

They kept rocking as Audrey said, "You believed I was involved in killing Lee Grimes."

"His note about knowing about the kid fooled me. I believed it could be you, but it was more likely that John's paternal grandfather arranged Lee's murder. I should have known you wouldn't be involved, and I owe you an apology. I'm sorry and I hope you'll forgive me."

She kept rocking but turned toward him. "What did I do to make you suspect me?"

Fen had to look away for a moment to gather his thoughts. "I live a solitary life on my ranch and go months without working a case. I wasn't prepared for attention from such a beautiful, smart, talented woman. A look in the mirror shows me a man on the downhill side of forty. I couldn't believe a woman like you would enjoy my company. The cop in me shouted, 'Watch out, Fen. It's a trap.'"

Audrey glanced over at him. "Sheriff Maguire, you need a new mirror. You took my breath away the first time I saw you. I'm having a hard time getting it back, even after what happened yesterday."

They rocked in silence, then Audrey asked, "When did you know Clayton Fox is my biological father?"

"Not for a long time. I thought the three tractors represented John, you, and John's paternal grandfather. It took many hours of staring at *Generations*. It was one of those moments when everything fell into place."

"Like what?"

"You're an attorney who specializes in family law. In law school, you learned a thing or two about concealing the identity of your son's father. I think you reverse-engineered the process and found your birth parents."

Audrey gave her head a weak nod. "Mom was easy. She died giving me life, then I was adopted by a wonderful childless couple. They still own a ranch near Brownwood. But that wasn't enough for me. Practicing family law and my own experience with an unplanned pregnancy messed with my mind. I developed an unhealthy curiosity to know my father. You discovered him in less than a week; it took me much longer, but I eventually found him. I moved to Smithville to be near my father and grandmother."

Fen said, "That's why you volunteered to work cattle with him on his ranch. Does he know you're his daughter?"

"No. And he's not going to."

Fen gave her his most serious look. "I didn't betray you yesterday and I never will."

Her chin quivered. "Thank you."

He moved on. "Your green eyes were also a clue to me. Your grandmother Mildred's are green. They don't sparkle like yours, but I bet they did when she was younger."

Audrey countered with, "You're quite the sleuth aren't you? All the photos in the yearbook are black and white, but you can tell my birth mother was blond. Green-eyed blonds are rare and my father's eyes are very dark. Most detectives wouldn't have put it together."

Fen nodded. "You have dark hair like your father, which was another clue."

Audrey ceased her rocking and looked at him for a long moment. "It's going to take a while for me to forgive you for putting my father in prison and having my grandmother arrested."

Fen stopped his rocking. "How long?"

"I don't know, five, ten, maybe fifteen years."

He blurted out, "Six years. I talked to Sally this morning. She gave me six more years to play widower-detective."

Audrey's gaze snapped up from watching a squirrel in the yard and met his. "What?"

"Six years. By then John will be a busy attorney with a wife and a baby. Bailey will be well on her way to becoming a successful artist." He paused, watching a yellow leaf fall to the ground. He brought his gaze back to her, brown eyes locking with green. "You're not the only one who's afraid of growing old alone."

The two started rocking again at the same moment. Audrey asked, "Is there a nice view from your back porch?"

"Breathtaking. There'll be a rocking chair waiting for you, right next to mine."

I hope you enjoyed your trip to the small town of Smithville in *Murder On The Colorado*. As with all the books in this series, I try to leave the reader with a feel for the local area, its beauty and attractions. However, with this book, I needed to take a little more fictional license to make the story work for my characters.

When my wife and I arrived at The Katy House Bed & Breakfast, I knew I had to write it into the story. My description of it in the book does not do it justice. Tiffany and Joe, the owners, have done an amazing job of bringing in modern conveniences while leaving the turn-of-the-century charm. And the breakfast... let's just say you won't find a better meal at a five star restaurant.

After learning I was writing a mystery set along the Colorado, Tiffany very graciously gave me her permission to use The Katy House name. My fictional license came in regard to Eloise, the owner in the book. Tiffany is very much a hands-on hostess, but I needed to take the fictional owner out of the story with her accident so I could bring Thelma in for a larger role. But just so you know... Tiffany would never leave her B&B in the hands of others, not even a real-life Fen Maguire! I apologize Tiffany and Joe, and thank you for your gracious consent to make the B&B such an integral part of this book.

If you enjoyed this book, please consider leaving a review at your favorite retailer, Bookbub or Goodreads. *Your* review could be the one that helps another reader discover their next great mystery!

To get in on the fun in my reader community, scan below or go to brucehammack.com/the-fen-maguire-mysteries-prequel/ to join my mailing list and receive a free copy of the series prequel, *Murder On Shinbone Creek.*

Happy Reading!
Bruce

See The Katy House Bed & Breakfast at katyhouse.com. Maybe even book a couple of nights in the Texas Special and experience the charm of Smithville for yourself.

You can learn more about Smithville and its connection to the movie, *Hope Floats,* at
https://gov.texas.gov/film/trail/smithville-texas.

Drawing from his extensive background in criminal justice, Bruce Hammack writes contemporary, clean read detective and crime mysteries. An avid Hercule Poirot and Sherlock Holmes fan, he believes the world can never have too many whodunits!

He is the author of the Smiley and McBlythe Mysteries, the Fen Maguire Mysteries, the Star of Justice series and the Detective Steve Smiley Mysteries. Having lived in eighteen cities around the world, he now shares his home in the Texas hill country with his wife of thirty-plus years.

Follow Bruce on Bookbub or Goodreads for the latest new release info and recommendations. Learn more at brucehammack.com.

www.ingramcontent.com/pod-product-compliance
Lightning Source LLC
Chambersburg PA
CBHW031441200726
48289CB00007BB/2065